Falling for ELLEN

KAITLIN COLLINS

Paperback ISBN-13: 979-8-9923956-3-1

Cover design by: Kaitlin Collins

Printed in the United States of America

To those who long to be loved for exactly who they are.

Prologue

Fergus

I knew my mind was failing me. I'd known before the doctors had given me my diagnosis, but had refused to acknowledge it. Of course, Alzheimer's makes itself harder and harder to ignore as time goes on.

Amidst the terror and frustration, I'd managed to find a few bright spots to the disease. There were books I knew I'd read before based on the notes tucked between the pages, that I now had the ability to read again and experience the story as if it were my first time; something any avid reader wished for when it came to their most beloved books.

Most importantly, there were times when my dear Ellen was still alive. Times when I did not remember her passing or the years of her fighting cancer. While our family and friends had seen the strong exterior she always portrayed, I had been the sole witness of her weakest and most vulnerable moments in the confines of our home.

Instead, when I awoke to find the bed next to me empty, my mind believed it was because Ellen— always the early riser—had already joined our neighbor in her garden for morning tea. Soon enough, the front door would open and she'd stride in and regale me with the inane gossip Sorcha had shared. Ellen would roll her eyes at the old busy body as if she wasn't interested in the clishmaclaver and I'd just smile back knowingly, allowing her the small white lie.

On those mornings, when I awoke unaware of reality, it was much easier to get out of bed on my own.

I thought my grandson, Alec's, idea of writing down my memories of Ellen was wonderful. I would

inevitably forget her at some point. However, if I had
our story written down, I would be able to read it and
fall in love with her all over again. As if experiencing
it all for the first time.

Alec's lassie, Lydia, claimed the armchair next to
mine, the blue leather journal she'd gifted me last
Christmas perched in her lap and pen at the ready.
The leather was the exact same shade of blue as
Ellen's eyes. There couldn't have been a more perfect
notebook to capture our story within.

Lydia's body radiated eagerness as she turned
herself towards me, her green eyes as bright as the
Highland hills in spring. "Alright. Let's start with the
first time you met Ellen."

I laughed at the memory and settled back into
my seat. The fire crackled in the hearth before us,
and I gazed into the flames as I let my mind wander
back to that fateful day.

"It was my third year at the University of
Edinburgh..."

Chapter 1

Fergus

September 1961

I sucked in a deep breath, relishing the scent of mahogany shelves crammed full of dusty textbooks and novels. The library was by far my favorite place on campus. I'd discovered a table tucked in a back corner away from the others my first year and had sat at it every day since, spending three hours studying or working on assignments. While having peace and quiet was extremely important, what had really sold me on the location was the floor to ceiling window that bathed the area in warmth on sunny days. Even on those rainy Scotland days, the patter of raindrops against the window panes was soothing and served as white noise while I toiled away. It was my quiet reprieve from the hustle and bustle of university life.

My footsteps came to a sudden halt as I rounded the corner, blinking several times to make sure I was seeing correctly. Sunlight streamed through the window, pouring over the dark wood table and...a head of raven hair.

My sanctuary had been tainted.

I could hardly see my beloved table beneath the nest of papers and books she'd created, clearly having made herself at home. Amidst it all were multiple different writing utensils. I always had three pens on me, but two pens and four pencils—one of which didn't even have an eraser—seemed excessive. The unnecessary clutter made my skin crawl. Not a hint of organization in sight.

I checked my timepiece, my chest pinching when I realized I'd already lost precious time trying to reconcile with what I'd found. It would take at least another five minutes to get her things gathered up and moved to another table. And that was being generous.

She was busy scribbling away in her notebook, so

I moved closer in hopes she'd hear my footsteps on the teakwood floor.

God, is that even English? How on earth is she able to read that?

If her utter disarray of materials wasn't enough to set my teeth on edge, her chicken scratch of handwriting surely did me in.

I cleared my throat, but she didn't immediately lift her head or even startle. Instead, she finished the sentence with an overly-punctuated period and then leisurely turned her head to look up at me.

"Can I help ye? I am in the middle of my essay," she sighed.

"Sorry to bother ye," I apologized quickly. "But...you are at my table."

Her eyebrows rose momentarily before she glanced around, even ducking down to look under the table—for what I hadn't a clue. Maybe she had dropped something and needed to gather it before relocating. But then she sat up and looked at me with that same dull look.

"I dinna see a name on it and there's no reservation sign to be found. So, I'm afraid this isna your table today."

A flush crept up the back of my neck and I rubbed

my hand over the warm skin. I was being kind. She was the one inconveniencing *me*.

"I have been sittin' at this table for the last three years, every day at this time to study," I tried explaining. "If ye'd just move to a different table, I'll help–"

"I'm not moving. Best ye find another table and leave me be."

My skin prickled with annoyance. It was a simple fix. Just a shuffling of papers and a couple trips across the aisle with an armful of books and she'd be settled in at another table and I'd be able to get back to my routine.

Her eyes stayed locked on mine, a calm and cool dark blue like the bottom of a loch. Aye, but the monster, Nessie, was clearly lurking in those depths.

I let out a huff. If I had any hopes of getting work done today, my only choice was to do as she said. I had already wasted precious time when the library was the quietest. I hefted my bag further onto my shoulder and turned on my heel for the table across the way, disappointed to find the sun had already abandoned this side of the room. Dropping my books onto the wood, I didn't even care that they landed with a loud thump. I felt particularly petty and hoped it disturbed her enough to make her lose her focus. The heavy chair scraped across the floor as I pulled it back and then plopped down into it.

She was unfazed, though, not even sparing a single glance in my direction. I inadvertently gripped my notebook too hard as I removed it from my satchel, crimping the corner so badly it resembled the one she'd been—allegedly—writing in. Mentally apologizing to the notebook, I did my best to smooth out the crease as much as possible before opening to my latest page of notes.

We'd been assigned a novel in my Celtic Revivals course and I'd already read far past the required chapters for this week. I often lost track of how long I'd been reading. However, I risked spoiling parts for my classmates if I got too far ahead. Lord knew I wouldn't be able to keep from talking about all I had read during our class discussion. I went on tangents quite often if I was being honest with myself, but I couldn't help it; I loved literature.

I skimmed back through the chapters we'd been assigned before turning my attention to my notebook to jot down all of my thoughts. I easily filled up several pages. Afterwards, I went back through my notes and starred ones I found especially important to share tomorrow in class.

Out of the corner of my eye, I spotted a figure rounding the biology shelves. My best mate, Doug, moved with a purpose, but came to a startled stop when his gaze met mine. His green eyes darted to my usual table, brows furrowing at the sight of the dark-haired lass. Then he hurriedly strode over to my "new" table and slipped into the chair across from me.

"What the hell are ye doing over *here*?" he questioned, doing his best to whisper. Unlike myself, Doug had experienced plenty of run-ins with the crabbit, old librarian that had ended in him being chased out.

"My spot was taken when I arrived," I answered shortly, sending a quick glare across the aisle before looking back at Doug. I'd fill him in more when we were in the privacy of our home. "The better question is what are *you* doing here? I thought ye'd be home tonight. Couldn't this wait until then?"

He shook his head, "The football lads want an answer as soon as possible."

I eyed him warily, unsure of what the football team had to do with me. While Doug and I had grown up running through the fields of our village and playing catch, organized sports were never my cup of tea. Where Doug was the overly-excited extrovert, I preferred to keep my circle small.

"We wanted to celebrate the season starting and thought a party would be a great way. Seeing as how I'm one of the only lads not living in a dormitory, they asked if I'd host." He held up his hand to stop me before I could even open my mouth. "I told them I had to ask ye first. Plead my case to ye, really."

I sat back, folding my arms over my chest, and looked at him expectantly. Undaunted, Doug just grinned brightly back at me.

"I promise ye won't have to do a thing. Barry is providing the alcohol and I'll clean everything up after they leave."

"How many?" I asked.

"Roughly twenty or so lads. Not everyone on the team can make it, but I ken a few of them are bringing their lassies. And, of course, I invited Freya."

Doug and Freya had been going steady for over a year and he was completely smitten. Anyone with eyes could tell they would be married soon enough. She was the perfect partner for him; reining in his puppy-like eagerness when appropriate, but still encouraging his big dreams. I couldn't be happier for him.

"Fine," I allowed.

Doug almost jumped out of his seat with excitement, but quickly caught himself.

"Thank ye, Fergus! I'll get ye your favorite whisky," he promised.

I shook my head at him, but couldn't hide my amused smile.

"Ye got your answer, now leave me be," I waved him away. "I'll see ye for supper and I expect to see that bottle of whisky waiting on the table for me."

He just grinned. "On it."

With that, he stood and left just as quickly as he had come. Watching him disappear around the bookshelf, my eyes unwillingly wandered to the intruder still occupying my table. Somehow the chaos in front of her seemed to have grown, taking up more than half of the tabletop. I'd only taken out the necessities in hopes she would leave soon and I could take my rightful spot. Alas, that was not the case.

Doug's contagious positivity had brightened my mood considerably and I did my best not to allow her to bring me back down into those grumpy depths, returning to my novel and disappearing into another world. I read two more chapters before coming up for air. The view outside the window had grown completely dark as the sun had dipped behind the surrounding buildings. A glance at my wristwatch showed I only had a few minutes left of my set time here and so I began to pack up my things. Again, I was probably a bit more forceful than necessary— especially when pushing in my chair—but this was my last chance to needle the obstinate lass.

As composed as ever, she didn't even budge as I walked by. I couldn't stop myself from glancing at the table to see what she was so focused on. The papers surrounding her contained detailed drawings of the human anatomy with various notes jotted down around them in her rough script. A sketch of a man's abdomen cut open with all of his inner organs on display was particularly disturbing and I questioned if I wanted to bother with supper. That was more than enough to send me on my way, the image now branded in my mind's eye.

"Better luck tomorrow, eh?"

I could hear the smug smile in her voice. My fingers clenched tightly around the strap of my satchel as I pushed on, not about to give her the satisfaction of a response.

We'll see about that.

Chapter 2

Ellen

October

Growing up in the small Highland village of Beauly, I'd always been an outsider. My classmates found my interests in the natural world to be odd. Girls would run away screaming when I'd show them a field vole I'd captured just outside of the school house and the boys were warned by their parents to stay away from me.

What kind of wife would that Ellen McLean make?

I'd learned early on that it was best to keep to myself and stay within the bubble of safety my family provided. Hence my surprise when I was invited to a get-together just off campus by Freya, an English lass who lived on the same floor as me in Mason Hall.

On the first day of classes, she'd spotted me struggling up the stairs under a tower of textbooks and had offered to help. We'd developed a small friendship since then, chatting in the hall or in the common area while we waited for the phone. We really only knew the basics about each other, so if there was an opportunity to spend time with her and get to know her better, I was going to take it.

I pulled the slip of paper from my pocket once more to double check the address Freya had given me. Freya's boyfriend, Douglas, was the one hosting the get-together at his place, a couple blocks off campus. A handful of students were scattered on the stoop, making it quite easy to determine which row house it was. They listened as a brunette lad told a story so animatedly, he splattered whisky down the steps. I made sure to tuck myself against the railing as I went up, staying as far from him as I could until I was in the safety of the house.

I had barely stepped inside when I heard my name called in Freya's unmistakable English accent, saving me from having to search for her. She sat on the arm of the sofa next to who I assumed was her boyfriend. His blonde hair, a shade or two darker than hers, looked as though it had at one point in the day been slicked back, but was now trying to defy gravity. She tapped him on the shoulder a couple times as I approached, drawing his attention away from the football match on the television.

"Dougie, this is Ellen. She's a biomedical sciences major," she grinned proudly at me.

Instinctively, I straightened my spine, preparing for his reaction. I was used to men finding it odd that I was pursuing a major in the sciences, a field some believed women did not belong in.

Douglas' eyes were wide as he stood, but his smile made me hopeful he would not be like others. "Really?" he breathed. "And what are ye hoping to do for a career with that?"

My shoulders relaxed and a smile eased onto my own face. "I want to go into the medical research field. Specifically preclinical research."

I'd grown up with Mam's stories about her experiences as an army nurse during the Second World War. Da had strongly discouraged her from telling such gruesome stories to a young child, but I had hung on to every word, completely enraptured. There were things my mother had seen that I couldn't imagine.

Since then, there had been many advances in the medical field and I felt very passionately about being a part of it. It was exhilarating to think I could possibly find a solution for an illness or make a procedure more efficient.

"That's quite an honorable field to go into." Douglas' smile turned suddenly sheepish. "And here I am, just a boring history major looking at what's already happened."

"Oi, that's still very important. It's the historians who help us learn about medical procedures of the past," I assured him. "How else are we to improve if we dinna ken what's already been done?"

"If only the politicians were of the same mindset as you," he joked, earning a laugh from me and a playful eye-roll from Freya.

She had landed herself quite the lad; open-minded, kind, and sincere. She was too wonderful of a woman to settle for anything less.

"Och! Where are my manners?" Douglas scoffed at himself. "Can I get ye something to drink? The lads brought over more than enough."

I waved him off, "I can get it myself. I've already taken ye away from your match long enough. Just point me in the right direction."

Freya leaned around me. "The kitchen is through that doorway there. Help yourself to anything and if you'd like, I have a bottle of wine stashed in the fridge. Just don't let anyone else know," she winked.

"I will be as discreet as possible," I promised with a soft chuckle.

There was only one other lass in the kitchen getting a drink and I waited until she had left before peeking into the fridge. For being in a home shared by several men, it was surprisingly clean and organized. Freya's wine bottle was tucked behind the milk and a neat stack of leftover containers. I made sure I was still the sole occupant of the kitchen before I poured myself a glass, using the door as a shield should someone come in search of their own libations.

I appeared to be in the clear until I replaced the bottle and closed the fridge door to reveal a man standing behind it. I jumped a little, having not heard him enter the kitchen.

"Oh dear, I–"

My words quickly died on my tongue as I

properly took in my unexpected guest. I would recognize those dark blue eyes anywhere. Usually, they were staring daggers at me.

So much for thinking I had avoided the annoying bloke from the library for the day. His eyebrows had climbed halfway up his forehead and his mouth slacked open very unbecomingly.

"What are *you* doing here?" he asked accusatorily.

I bristled instantly and then straightened to my full height. However, it only brought me up to eye level with his chin.

"My friend, Freya, invited me," I answered curtly.

His eyebrows were practically at his hairline now, partially hidden under the messy curls falling over his forehead. Normally, he looked much more put together when I saw him in the library, his dark hair slicked back with pomade.

"F-Freya. As in Doug's Freya?"

"Well, she isna his property, but she is his girlfriend, aye." In order to avoid any further ignorant questions, I continued on. "We live on the same floor and met at the beginning of the semester. Suppose I could ask why *you* are here."

The infamous scowl of his returned, lips pulling down into a deep frown and brows lowering.

"I live here."

I had nothing else to say to him, however; he was currently in the doorway, removing any possible exit for myself that didn't include brushing past this bampot of a man. So, I simply averted my gaze and took a sip of my wine as I leaned against the counter, the picture of indifference.

"Ah, so Freya let ye into her secret stash, eh? Or did ye sneak in there yourself? It does seem to be a trend of yours to take things that dinna belong to ye." I could hear the taunting sneer in his voice, but I didn't grant him a response.

"Oh, Fergus! I see you've met Ellen," Freya smiled as she slipped in around his shoulder.

So, the irritating bloke has a name, then. Fergus.

"I see ye've let her into your secret stash," was his quick response.

Freya picked up on the tone of his voice and turned from getting her own glass to eye the two of us. I did my best to look as cordial as possible.

"Do you two know each other?"

I looked expectantly at him, waiting to see what

he would say. Did Freya and Douglas already know about the girl who stole his table in the library? His eyes just stayed locked on mine.

"Aye, a little. I ken her from studying in the library."

If Freya knew anything, she didn't let it show. She simply filled up her glass and tucked the wine back into its designated corner of the fridge behind the milk before hooking her arm through mine.

"Well, if you don't mind, I'm going to steal her and introduce her to Malcolm and Boyd. Dougie says they're both science majors like Ellen, here." She waved her hand towards the living room. "He's watching the match if you need him."

Fergus nodded in acknowledgement and then stepped to the side so he was no longer blocking the doorway. I could feel his eyes burning into me as we walked past, knowing the sensation all too well. While the idea of being introduced to two science blokes sounded about as enjoyable as having a root canal with no anesthesia, it was much more preferable than staying in the kitchen with *Fergus*.

"I suppose that puts a spanner in my plan to get you and Fergus together," Freya sighed heavily.

If I'd had a mouthful of wine, I would have surely

spat it out all over the hall. Although the idea of Fergus' reaction to red wine stains everywhere was quite appealing.

"Excuse me. What?" I stared at her with wide eyes.

Freya just shrugged as she moved closer to me to slip past two lads yelling at the television.

"I love Fergus and I never mind when he joins myself and Dougie for nights out, but I always feel so bad for him. It can't be fun tagging along with a couple all the time." She finally looked at me. "After meeting you, I had the brilliant idea of introducing you to each other. With him and Doug being friends and you and I being friends, it just seemed like the perfect solution. But based on his behavior just then, I'm thinking I might've been incorrect in that assumption."

It suddenly felt very hot in the cramped house and I took a step away from Freya to escape the warmth of her body pressed against my side. I took a giant gulp of my wine, not even tasting the scarlet liquid. I'd only ever been someone's girl once and it had ended so brutally, I didn't have any inclination to try it again.

"Ellen?" Freya's voice sounded echoey and far

away. I forced myself to focus on her and take a deep breath to calm my pounding heart. "Are you alright?"

"Yes, sorry. Just…"

How did I explain to Freya how I felt about relationships? How my sole experience with one made me jaded because in the end, it had all been a lie? Were we at that level of friendship, yet? I didn't know how these sorts of things worked.

"I'm not looking for a relationship. I've got to stay focused on my academics and my career after that," I finally managed.

Freya's smile was gentle as she reached out for me once more and gave my arm a gentle squeeze. "Of course. As I said, it was just a thought."

I nodded, feeling a bit steadier now. We'd made it to the door and I welcomed the fresh air on my clammy skin, no matter how cold it might be. The group of students on the stoop turned at our appearance and when Freya introduced Malcolm, she pointed to the man who had been spilling whisky all over with his gesticulations. Why was I not surprised?

Chapter 3

Fergus

I sat at the kitchen table, content to enjoy my toast and coffee while I watched Doug throw discarded beer bottles into a bin bag. After waking up and seeing the mess his teammates had left last night, I was more than happy to cash in on his offer to clean up.

"Wait. Let me get this straight." Doug paused in the middle of the kitchen and shook his head back and forth as if clearing away cobwebs. "Ellen is the lass that's been drivin' ye absolutely mad the last few weeks? But she was so nice and interesting to talk to."

I let out a huff and grumbled, "Well ye werena

tryin' to tell her to move her things to another table."

"Are ye sure ye didn't just start off on the wrong foot? Maybe ye came off a little strong. I mean, it is just a table."

"It's not *just* a table. It's the best spot to study in the entire library." I started ticking off attributes on my fingers. "Out of view of the information desk, restrooms just around the corner, but most importantly, the wi-"

Doug rolled his eyes. "Aye, the window. I hear ye."

He wasn't even fazed by my glare as I stood to refill my coffee. When I sat back down, the chair creaked underneath me and I said a quick, silent prayer for it to hold up for another day. The poor dining set had already been on its last leg when we purchased it from the secondhand store—we were only two lads in uni after all—and despite Doug's best efforts to reinforce the chairs, they were still quite questionable.

"I asked her politely if she would switch tables. *She* was the one who got in a tizzy and was rude."

"Yes, but...I ken how ye can get when it comes to your routine. I learned a long time ago not to interfere with it. Can ye no share the space? Surely there's enough room for the two of ye."

"I'd thought of that, but her things take up the entire table, all spread out as she has them." I didn't mention that the contents of her books made me nauseous, and I preferred to be nowhere near them.

Doug rubbed the spot between his eyebrows. I knew he was genuinely trying to help and I couldn't fault him for it.

"Maybe Freya can talk to her," he offered with a sigh, his last-ditch effort.

Just from what I knew about the lass based on the few interactions we'd had, I didn't see even sweet Freya being able to change her mind. At least not about giving up my table.

"If she could at least have a schedule instead of just randomly being there, that'd be better," I muttered, compromising somewhat. For Doug's sake, of course.

He tied up the bin bag. "I'll suggest that."

The clock in the living room chimed the hour and Doug grabbed the two bags he'd managed to fill.

"I've got to pick up Freya from Masson Hall. Promised I'd give her a ride to her job, so I'll try and bring it up on the way. Otherwise, she's coming over tonight if that's alright with ye?"

I nodded, taking the last bite of my toast and dusting the crumbs from my fingers. "Of course. Ye ken I'm always happy to see Freya. Even if she is a Sassenach," I winked at him.

"Ye'll never let her live it down, will ye?" He shook his head, but he was smiling at me.

"Nor you. You're the one who's dating a Brit after all. Such a disappointment to your fellow Scots."

Doug made sure one of the bags knocked into my shoulder as he passed, successfully spilling some of my coffee. Thankfully, it landed on the table and not on my lap, only adding to the numerous stains in the old wood. We were both muffling smiles as we glanced over our shoulders at each other before he headed out the door.

While my weeks were occupied with classes and studying in the library, I spent my weekends working at a bookshop nearby. A very stereotypical occupation for an English major, but I always had first access to new inventory.

The air was extremely damp when I stepped out of the house, tucking my hands into my pockets. The clouds hung low and full; a harbinger of the long weeks of rain to come. I ducked back in momentarily to grab my umbrella perched behind the door. It was highly likely I'd be needing it for the walk home later.

It seemed most everyone else was staying shut in, the streets not as busy as usual at this time of day. I enjoyed the abnormal quiet on my short walk, but was more than happy to get out of the chill and step into the warmth of the shop. The bell above the door rang cheerfully to announce my arrival.

I paused in the entry, taking a moment to breathe in that special smell that only belongs to libraries and bookstores; the comforting aroma of fresh pages and ink. There was no place I felt more at home than amongst stacks of books.

I didn't miss the hint of coffee wafting towards me from the office and found myself wandering in that direction as if my feet had a mind of their own. Another cup couldn't hurt. Mr. Graham was prepared for me, already having filled two mugs.

He turned and smiled at me from behind his spectacles. "Aye, right on time as always, Fergus."

I took a seat at the small table and he slid one of the mugs across to me.

"I appreciate ye, Mr. Graham," I smiled gratefully.

He sipped on his own, the white whiskers of his

mustache slightly tinted by the dark brown liquid when he lowered his cup. With the matter of caffeine settled, I could see his gears turning as he determined what needed to be done for the day.

"We got a new shipment in this morn, so I'd like ye to go through it and sort the books. Then the children's section always needs straightening."

Reorganizing the children's section was a daily chore. Not that I could hold it against the wee bairns for struggling to put the books back in their rightful places. The sticky fingerprints, though? The bane of my existence.

With the day laid out for me, I downed the rest of my coffee and then set off for the backroom where Mr. Graham kept the extra inventory. Content in the company of only books, I settled in amongst the boxes and began sorting. I recognized several of the titles and the ones I wasn't familiar with, I flipped through to read a couple pages. By the time my stomach started growling, I had only one box left and was surrounded by multiple piles. One specifically being the pile of books I wanted for my own personal library. Of course, I'd have to go back through and narrow it down to only a few or Doug would have my head.

Like any book lover, my dream was to one day have a library within my own home like the one I had growing up. Mam was quite the bookworm and Da was all too happy to build her shelves and fill them with all the books she could ever want. Then when my siblings and I came along, some of the lower shelves were dedicated to our books. My older brother grew out of it by the time he left primary school, but my sister and I stayed avid readers. More often than not, we could be found curled up in front of the hearth with a book.

Pulled from my thoughts by the incessant grumbling of my stomach, I stood and carefully picked my way through the piles to return to the storefront. Mr. Graham's signature tweed cap was easy to spot above some of the shorter bookshelves. Despite his age, he was just as involved in the maintenance of the store as anyone else and could be found stocking and rearranging shelves at any given moment.

"Mr. Graham, I'm going to the cafe for a sandwich and tea. Would ye like me to bring ye back anything?"

He didn't even turn. "The missus packed some food for me, but aye. I'll take a scone if ye don't mind."

"A scone it is," I confirmed with a chuckle to myself.

I went back to the office to grab my jacket before leaving the warmth of the shop. Even if I was only going across the street, the fog had settled into the city and there was no sense being chilled if I didn't have to be. Thankfully the cozy cafe was even warmer than the bookshop due to the coffee machines brewing and ovens running non-stop. It was reasonably busy, but the fair-haired lass behind the counter still welcomed me in the midst of helping another customer.

"Afternoon, Fergus!" Moira called out.

She was a sweet, young girl who'd been employed at the cafe almost as long as I'd been at the bookstore, working to save money for university.

"Afternoon, Moira. Keepin' busy I see."

She shrugged in a 'what can you do' way and turned her attention back to the customer, passing them a baggie full of their chosen baked goods. I grabbed a handful of napkins from the counter before I joined the queue and neatly folded them in half to tuck into my pocket. As soon as it was my turn, Moira just gave me a knowing look.

"The usual, I take it?"

I smiled sheepishly at her as I nodded. Okay, maybe I had a slight problem with routines and sticking too tightly to them, but they helped me stay organized and get my daily tasks done. If I spent too long trying to decide what to order, half of my break would have already passed before I'd even taken a bite.

"And a scone for Mr. Graham, if ye please." I gestured towards the display case, "Ye ken he'll enjoy whatever ye give him."

Her lips pursed as she stepped over to the case and eyed its contents before plucking an apple and butterscotch scone from its tray. "Clara has been creating new, autumn recipes. I think Mr. Graham will enjoy this one just fine," she smiled politely.

While she bagged it, I dug my wallet out and placed enough for the sandwich, tea, and scone on the counter.

"Thank ye, Moira. Keep the change for your college fund, aye?"

"Bless ye, Fergus," she smiled gratefully as she passed me the paper bag.

I moved to the side then to wait for my order, allowing the next customer to step up. The delicious scent wafting from the baggie in my hand had me wishing I had gotten a scone as well. This is what I got for never straying from my normal. Before I could fret over it for too long, Clara called my name for my bacon butty and tea. I thanked both women once again and bid them farewell, using my elbow to push the door open.

I hunched my shoulders up around my ears and made sure the road was clear before hurrying back across to the bookshop. Never had Mr. Graham turned so quickly at the sound of the bell above the door. I just smiled to myself and set down my tea on a shelf long enough to hand him the bag holding his scone once he'd stepped down from the ladder.

"Clara's apparently experimenting with new flavors, but Moira insisted ye'd like it."

He gave the scone a curious sniff and then his eyes widened slightly in what I assumed was interest. His expressions were often quite hard to read, hidden as they were behind his bushy eyebrows and thick beard.

"Smells like butterscotch," he hummed before retreating to the office to enjoy his treat.

I carefully picked up my cup to follow behind him when the bell announced the arrival of a customer. Turning to greet the newcomer, I almost dropped my tea when I found Ellen standing in the doorway.

I couldn't escape her. Was no place safe?

The tip of her nose was pink from the chill and her curls were frizzy, apparently not agreeing with the moisture in the air. She seemed just as displeased to see me, although I'd yet to see anything but a frown or smug smile on her face.

Knowing Mr. Graham would be able to hear me through the office's open door, I put on my best customer service voice and smiled as cordially as I could manage. "Welcome to Graham's Bookshop. Can I help ye find anything?"

One of her dark brows quirked up. "No. Thank ye. I'm sure I can manage on my own."

I shrugged, having no issues with leaving her to her own devices, and turned to retreat to the backroom to eat in peace. "There's a bell on the counter if ye need assistance."

I hurried past Mr. Graham in the office, needing to get to the backroom and as far away from her as possible. This was the third time she had encroached on a space of mine I considered to be sacred. My table, my *home*, and now my workplace? I didn't know who I'd pissed off to warrant this.

I bit into my bacon butty harsher than necessary, taking my frustration out on my poor lunch. I couldn't even enjoy Clara's delicious creation. I'd barely eaten half of my sandwich when I heard the wee bell on the counter chime brightly.

"Fergus, can ye get that?" Mr. Graham called, his voice muffled as if speaking around a mouthful of scone. At least someone was getting to enjoy their meal.

I grumbled a few curses under my breath before I managed to compose myself, straightening up and dusting any stray crumbs from my slacks. When I re-entered the storefront, Ellen was standing at the counter, still looking like a grumpy cat that'd gotten caught in the rain.

"I'm looking for *The Intelligent Man's Guide to Science* by Isaac Asimov." Saying the title out loud seemed to physically pain Ellen, her mouth twitching to the side as if the words tasted bitter on her tongue.

It was quite an unfortunate title given her circumstances. I could have easily used it to get a jab in against her, but I didn't feel comfortable doing so. Instead, I—momentarily—set our animosity aside and decided to behave as if she were any other customer.

"Let me check." I tilted my head towards our non-fiction section.

Ellen let out a heavy sigh as she followed behind me. "I haven't been able to find it anywhere else and we need it for class next week. Freya suggested I come here," she explained.

The book could be in a number of places if Mr. Graham had been the one who shelved it. I'd been slowly trying to redo his classification system, but it was still a work in progress. I checked the science shelves first.

Ellen stepped close to look as well and the scent of her perfume wrapped itself around me. It was floral, but nothing like the overly-flowery perfume my Gran would douse herself in. This was much sweeter.

Realizing I was just standing there smelling her, I took a large step away, using the excuse of continuing on to the research section. And yet, her scent still lingered.

"Ah. Here it is." I retrieved the book from one of the top shelves. "Must've been too high for you to see," I smiled smugly down at her, purposefully standing at my full height.

I couldn't have her thinking we were on good terms just because we had mutual friends. She was still a table thief and safe space invader.

Ellen's eyes narrowed as she snatched the book from my hands, but my smile just grew even more pleased. Without so much as a 'thank you', she turned and stalked over to the register, dropping the book to the counter more carelessly than necessary. Even if it did have a shite title, no book deserved to be treated that way.

Moving behind the counter, I quickly rang her up. When I handed back her change, I watched in mild horror as she hastily shoved the banknotes and coins into her pocket. This woman was a monster.

She seized the book off the counter and turned on her heel for the exit.

"Have a nice day!" I called out in an overly sweet voice.

I couldn't be sure, but I thought I at least got a grumble out of her. Or maybe it was more of a growl.

Chapter 4

Ellen

"You are a very talented student, Miss McLean. I cannot deny that. However, I am concerned the topic you have chosen for your essay is beyond even your scope of intellect."

I couldn't decide if it was my professor's curt Queen's English or his blatant misogyny that irked me more. While I was not the only female student enrolled in a sciences major, it was very clear to us we weren't exactly welcomed. I had the visceral urge to shove my rough draft down his throat. Even though I had strong reason to believe my brothers would greatly approve of my impulse, it would do myself—and the other women—no good if I handled this in the way I would like to.

Instead, I took a deep, steadying breath, giving myself time to come up with the "proper" response.

"I understand your concern, professor, and I appreciate it," I began, making sure to tame my Highland accent as much as possible. I'd gotten quite good at it over the past few years spent in Edinburgh. "However, I would also appreciate the opportunity to challenge myself. How am I to grow if I am always doing what is merely expected of me?"

I raised my dark brows slightly and was pleased when he opened his mouth only to close it again. He took off his glasses and absently rubbed at the bridge of his nose.

"If that is what you want. I will still be strict with my grading, so I want no complaints if you do not receive the score you are hoping for."

Continuing with my docile female façade, I just nodded, trying to look as grateful as possible. He dismissed me, and my mask dropped the second his office door closed behind me.

"Bloody fandan," I grumbled under my breath, stomping down the hall. "Thinks he kens what's in my 'scope of intellect'. Well, I ken that he's a bawbag."

My heartbeat pounded in my ears, and the heated flush in my cheeks told me my face was scarlet red. The audacity of men continued to astound me. Why was I even surprised anymore?

Adrenaline had been pumping through me since he'd pulled me aside after his lecture and asked me to come to his office. Talking one-on-one with an educator had never turned out well for me. Growing up, teachers would confiscate items I found and brought into class, such as feathers or insects collected in my empty milk bottle; they'd demand I be more ladylike when I got mud on my skirts from sitting in the dirt or skinned my knee climbing a tree to examine a starling's nest; and worst of all, they'd tawse the palm of my hands when they got tired of my antics.

I flexed my hands and then clenched them into fists as I recalled the sting of the leather. I had never let those teachers discourage me, and I wasn't about to start now. I would have to make my professor eat his words by writing the best academic essay possible.

It was only once I'd reached the library, secluding myself near the biology section, that I actually looked at the rough draft he'd returned to me. He'd made so many notes in his thick chicken scratch that my original words were barely legible. There was nothing for me to do but buckle down and get to work.

Before I knew it, I was drowning in a sea of textbooks, science journals, and medical history; the books towering precariously around me. Any piece of information that may somewhat support my theory, I'd scribbled down in my notebook. I'd have to organize it later, but I could do that in my dormitory at another time. The library only stayed open so late, and I'd already lost track of how long I'd been here.

My eyes were burning, and my body ached. I leaned back in the seat, having been hunched over, and stretched my arms above my head. My lower back popped audibly, but it felt so good I didn't care if anyone heard. Stretching my neck as well, I closed my eyes and enjoyed the small respite. Sheer anger and determination could only last so long in one sitting.

Suddenly, a flash of lightning lit up the dark library, soon followed by thunder that rattled the window panes. Within seconds, raindrops were pelting the glass, and my moment of peace was over.

"Shite," I muttered.

When it rains, it pours. Today was just not my day in the slightest. Stupid me hadn't thought to grab my umbrella on the way out; an absolute rookie mistake given it was October in Scotland. There were only so many places to take cover on the way from the library to my dormitory. No matter what, I would end up completely drenched, and with my luck, catch a cold to boot.

I could only hope the storm was a short one and would blow through by the time I finished. It was almost three o'clock, which meant I still had roughly four hours before the librarian would start closing the library and shoving us out the door.

Just as I flipped to a fresh page in my notebook, the screech of chair legs on the wooden floor set my teeth on edge and my body instantly tensed up once more. I didn't even have to look to know it was Fergus. Rarely did anyone ever sit down over here. Any disturbance came from the rare biology student retrieving books from the shelves and then retreating back to their table elsewhere.

"Can ye not be so obnoxious for one day, please?" I hissed.

His head snapped up, eyes already narrowed at

me. "Can ye not steal my table for one day?" he countered.

My blood reached boiling temperatures once more and I had to force myself to keep my voice down, but I didn't hold back on the disdain and aggravation I felt.

"It isna your goddamn table!" I snapped at him.

He opened his mouth to respond, but the sound of the librarian scolding another student nearby stopped him. Instead, he leveled me with a glare that I heartily returned. I didn't blink until he finally gave in and looked away. It was a minor victory, but today? I would take any win I could get.

Feeling obscenely petty, especially in regards to annoying men, I made sure to purposefully open my textbook with more force than necessary, resulting in a satisfying thud as the hardcover met the wooden tabletop. No other disruptions came from Fergus' direction, so I reverted all my attention to the task at hand: to prove my professor wrong.

The click of the librarian's heels announced her presence before her voice did; otherwise, I might have jumped at the sudden disruption.

"The library will be closing. I need the both of you to put away your materials or leave them in an orderly pile," she requested before continuing her rounds. While her tone had been polite, I knew she was a no-nonsense woman and would not stand for a student leaving a mess behind.

It surprised me to find Fergus still at the table across from me. Normally, he only stayed until six, and then he was gone, on the dot, without fail. A quick glance around showed that we were some of the only ones left in the library, this area barely lit by our two lone lamps.

His workspace was much more organized than mine, with just a few books and his notebook. Which reminded me I had quite the mess to clean up and not much time to do so before the librarian returned.

There was no way I had enough time to place all the books in their rightful spots on the shelves, so I grouped them the best I could to match the library's classification system. Then I gathered my notes and rough draft to tuck into my satchel, donning my coat over the top to add an extra layer of protection against the rain. The last thing I needed was for my essay to get wet and the ink to bleed after I'd spent all afternoon and evening on it.

The storm had not let up in the slightest, the rain coming down in sheets of fat drops. All I could do was stare out at the campus lawn with a deeply etched frown. Even with my coat and leather satchel providing a barrier, the rain would surely seep through both by the time I got to Masson Hall.

Another rumble of thunder made me wince. I'd developed a massive headache at some point, most likely from going without eating since my measly breakfast of a singular bannock and tea. At the reminder, my stomach gave a growl to rival the thunder's roar.

Between the two, I didn't hear my name called until the person was standing right beside me. It took me a moment to place who it was, given that they were merely a silhouette backlit by the library's interior lights, but then lightning illuminated his face long enough for me to recognize his scowl. Fergus.

"Do ye not have an umbrella?" he asked, sounding a bit more upset with me than I thought was warranted.

What did it have to do with him? He was clearly prepared, opening his own umbrella above his head for the trek across campus. Instead of snipping back at him and saying as much, I just shook my head. I'd fought enough impertinent men today.

He glanced around the campus and then back at me before he offered out his arm. "Let me walk ye to your dormitory."

I just stared at the proffered arm as if it were a foreign object. A slimy tentacle, perhaps. Fergus made an impatient noise.

There was only one dormitory for women on campus, and he knew I lived there, same as Freya. Normally, the walk took me a mere ten minutes, but trudging through a storm and puddles that came up to my ankles would make the going a bit more difficult. Truthfully, I didn't have much of a choice. If I didn't want to be drenched in seconds flat and walk into my dorm looking like a drowned rat with disintegrating papers in my satchel, my only option was to walk with him under the safety of his umbrella.

"Okay," I mumbled out, unsure if he could hear me over the storm's rumbling.

I slipped my hand into the crook of his arm as we descended the stairs. Raindrops trickled off the side of the umbrella and onto my shoulder, so I huddled even closer. He smelled of wet wool and wood smoke, a somehow comforting blend. Maybe because it reminded me of the sheep back home in Beauly and spending a rainy evening warming my toes by the hearth.

"Ye don't have to do this," I protested lightly.

"Freya would have my heid if she found out I'd let ye walk home in an evendoun pour such as this."

I couldn't help but chuckle a little to myself at the sudden mental image of Freya going after Fergus.

The going was awkward. Within seconds, my heels resembled two small lochs, and my feet kept slipping inside the wet leather. One particular step caused me to clutch Fergus' arm tighter in order to keep from rolling my ankle. He came to an abrupt stop, his free hand resting on top of mine as I steadied myself.

"Sorry," I blurted.

How on earth was his hand so warm? I was freezing all over.

"Are ye alright?" It was the most concern I'd ever heard in his voice.

He looked me over, lingering on my heels, the clear culprit. My cheeks flushed like some regency debutant with the local rake eyeing my scantily exposed ankles.

"Fine," I choked out, beginning to walk again. "It's just a little slippery."

Once we reached the pavement at the main road, Fergus removed his arm from my grasp to switch the umbrella to his other hand and nudged me towards the opposite side of him with a hand on the small of my back. A shock of electricity shot up my spine as if I'd been struck by lightning. It took everything in me not to shy away like a skittish horse.

"Dinna want a car to hit a puddle and douse ye," he explained casually.

I managed a soft thank you, barely audible over the pounding of the rain on the umbrella's canvas. Having switched sides, I tried my best to adjust my satchel under my coat so it was between me and Fergus and thus completely covered. It was at that moment my heel decided to slide almost completely off. We halted once more.

"Agh!" I groaned, glaring down at the offending footwear as I attempted to right it.

"Are ye hungry?" Fergus asked suddenly.

Maybe my stomach's growls hadn't blended in with the sounds of the storm as much as I'd thought. With my shoe successfully on—for now—I looked up to meet his gaze.

"Actually, yes," I admitted. "I only had time for breakfast today."

Fergus took a moment to look around. "There's a restaurant just down this block. I'd kill for a bowl of hot soup at the moment if ye'd like to join."

I practically moaned at the idea of soup and a warm cup of tea. We'd barely made it off campus, and I was already chilled to the bone.

"That sounds marvelous," I agreed.

I could've sworn I saw an actual smile on his face, but it could have been a trick of the light. He checked both ways before assisting me across the street. I just prayed that I didn't lose a shoe in the middle of the road. We ducked under awnings when we could, but the restaurant wasn't far at all, and there were no other footwear fiascos on my part.

Fergus stepped to the side as he opened the door and held the umbrella over me until I'd made it safely inside. I didn't realize how tense I'd been until I stepped into the warmth and felt my muscles loosen in relief. A warm meal would have me thawing out in no time.

Despite, or because of, the gloomy weather, the restaurant was still fairly busy. University students were scattered about, either studying through their supper or enjoying a meal with friends. A group of men in the corner was sharing stories, laughing boisterously. Fortunately, the sole empty table was on the other side of the room from them. Even better was its proximity to the fire burning in the hearth. The universe was apparently apologizing for this miserable day.

We quickly snagged the table and had just sat down when a waitress appeared to get our drink order.

"Chamomile tea, please," I requested. I'd need the help falling asleep tonight after the afternoon I'd had. Knowing my brain, it'd be racing with ideas for my essay and not-so-kind thoughts about my professor.

"Coffee for me," Fergus ordered.

I raised a brow at him, "Coffee at this hour?"

"Had the library not closed, I would've still been there," he explained. "I have a manuscript I'm writing. I haven't quite finished the first draft yet, and it can be hard to focus when Doug has Freya over."

"I'm quite shocked ye broke your precious routine. Normally, you're out of there by six."

His brows shot up. "You noticed my schedule?"

He smirked across the table at me as he reclined back in his chair, stretching his long legs out in front of him. Oh, to be a man who could take up as much space as he wanted. Refusing to shrink for him, I stretched my legs out as well, crossing them at my ankles. What I really wanted was to kick off my soaked shoes and let my feet breathe. I'd be lucky if I didn't end up with trench foot.

"Well, it's quite difficult to concentrate when someone is trying to murder me with their eyeballs," I quipped, raising my own brows in return. "I practically count down the minutes 'til ye leave."

Fergus actually laughed at that; a sound I'd never heard from him. The waitress appeared then with our steaming mugs, momentarily interrupting the conversation as she placed them in front of us. I scanned the menu quickly.

"I'll have the Cullen Skink. Biggest bowl ye've got," I ordered, practically salivating at the mere idea of the hearty dish.

"Actually, I'll have the same," Fergus decided.

He smiled politely up at her as he handed back the menus. We each took a sip of our drinks, conversation lulling for just a moment. The hot tea burned its way down my throat and into my stomach, beginning to thaw me from the inside out.

"Are ye writin' a book then?" I inquired, referring back to his mention of a manuscript.

"Aye," he nodded. "A mostly fictional piece that takes place during the Great War. Much of it is based on my own da's experience as a soldier."

I shifted forward without even realizing it, my interest piqued. "My mam was a nurse during the war."

"Really?" Fergus perked up as well. "Has she told ye stories?'

"Oh plenty! They're the reason I want to go into biomedical sciences. The procedures she witnessed are so fascinating."

As a little girl, I'd listened as she told of nurses using their own hair for sutures or stethoscopes as drips. She'd described in detail the new methods of treatments that had been discovered, like the removal of dead and damaged tissue to prevent infection or using metal plates to secure bones and improve healing time. I'd hung onto every word.

"Do ye think she'd mind sharing her stories with me and possibly answering some questions?" Fergus asked, a hopeful look in his blue eyes.

"She wouldna mind at all. I can ask when I call her this weekend."

Saturday mornings were for phone calls back home and catching up on what my parents and brothers were up to.

"Thank ye, Ellen," Fergus smiled genuinely. "I appreciate it."

I bowed my head once and then used my cup to hide the light blush on my cheeks as I took a sip. Maybe I could blame it on the chill, even though I had warmed up significantly in our time here.

Our soups arrived then, and we ate in companionable silence. It took everything in me not to groan in appreciation. It had to have been the creamiest Cullen Skink I'd ever had, with just the right amount of smoky flavor from the haddock. How had I lived just blocks from this place for nearly three years and never stopped in?

By the time I finished, I was pleasantly warm both inside and out and had practically melted into the chair. I felt like a fat house cat curled up in front of the hearth. In fact, sleep might come easier tonight than I had even hoped for.

"Shall I get ye home then?" Fergus finally spoke up, setting his spoon in his empty bowl.

I looked to the window where the rain continued to come down in dredges and couldn't help but grimace. The last thing I wanted to do was leave the cozy bubble we were in and trudge through the wet cold once more.

"Or not yet, I suppose," Fergus chuckled. I turned my gaze back to him, confused by what he meant. "Ye look fairly content."

I couldn't argue with that. This was the most relaxed I'd felt since the semester had started. Most shocking about it all was my current company. Fergus had been the source of half my headaches the last few months, and yet here I was, willingly spending time with him.

"I am." I sighed, "It's been a long day."

He hummed a little in thought as he stroked his thumb along the handle of his mug. "Ye did seem a bit more on edge than usual this afternoon. Anything in particular got ye feeling so cross?"

The nasty pit in my stomach tried to return as I thought back on the conversation with my professor. "Just my misogynistic professor sharing his unwanted opinions with me," I muttered, the words flying out without much thought. They weren't a lie, though.

Fergus let out an amused sort of noise from the back of his throat, and I caught a hint of a smile at the corner of his lips.

"Quite the foolish man, then, is he?" When I just stared at him, he continued on. "I have more than enough personal experience to ken ye are not one to be trifled with."

"I'm going to take that as a compliment."

"As ye should."

The gentle curve in his lips and warmth in his eyes unnerved me, the expression foreign on his face, especially when directed at me. So, I averted my eyes back to the window and found it had slowed to a mere drizzle outside.

"Think we should take advantage of the break?" I asked Fergus.

We could only stay for so long. Eventually, the restaurant would need to close, and I was more than ready to curl up in my bed under the quilt and drift off to dreamland.

He followed my gaze. "Best not press our luck, aye?"

My heels let out a horrendous squelch when I stood, and I grimaced. I could tell Fergus was muffling a laugh as he led me to the door. He stepped out first, making sure to have the umbrella open for me even though the rain had lessened.

"Ye dinna have to walk me home, now. Promise I willna melt."

He simply shrugged, something he seemed to do often. "It's not much further to Masson Hall, and you're basically on my way."

Having been to his and Douglas' house now, I knew it very much was not on his way, but I wasn't about to argue. I didn't have much fight left in me today, and he would only be inconveniencing himself, so I fell into step beside him.

The evening had taken quite a shocking turn. Had someone told me I would be having supper with Fergus, I would have laughed in their faces. A full witchy cackle. But I'd actually found myself enjoying the time spent with him. It could've just been the delicious meal, though, and how desperate I was to be somewhere warm and dry.

Yes, that was it. Any company would have been tolerable in the state I'd been in; famished and soaked to the bone. I may have even been able to eat supper with one of the bigots from my classes. Maybe.

It was just a few blocks to Masson Hall, and I had never been so excited to see the building. All the warmth I'd accumulated at the restaurant had quickly dissipated in the damp air, and the soles of my feet were painfully wrinkled at this point. Fergus followed me all the way up the steps to the door. I turned and sent him a polite smile.

"Well...thank ye for walking me. I'm significantly drier than I would have been, and ye saved my research." I patted my dry satchel underneath my coat.

He waved me off. "It was nothing. Thank ye for joining me for supper."

I acknowledged him with a nod, and then we both just stood there. I shifted my weight before clearing my throat, the atmosphere suddenly very awkward.

"Goodnight then, Fergus." I reached for the handle of the door, and he stepped back to give me room to open it.

Then he bowed his head slightly. "Goodnight, Ellen."

He went back down the stairs to the pavement,

and I found myself watching him until he disappeared around the corner. Even as I stepped inside, his presence lingered, like a phantom limb still aching after amputation.

Chapter 5

Fergus

November

One of my professors had agreed to meet with me outside of his office hours to review what I had so far of my manuscript. The first draft was finished, but it was bare bones with all things considered. There was still plenty for me to improve upon and add to make it a quality piece of literature.

Getting more firsthand accounts of the war from those who had experienced it would help with that. The week after I'd walked her home, I'd come across Ellen in the library—once again at my table. She'd paused her studies long enough to let me know her mother would be happy to speak to me. She gave me the number to call and then went back to her paper without another word.

While it wasn't the warmest interaction, it was still better than our usual, and with all the stress we'd both been under, it seemed our little rivalry could be set to the side. For now, at least.

Reaching the office, I rapped my knuckles against the door frame so as not to startle Professor Campbell. He was quite young in comparison to most of the other educators here at the university, somewhere in his fifties. Still, he wore spectacles with the thickest lenses I believe I'd ever seen. When he peered up from the book on his desk, he looked like a goldfish, irises as big as a five-pound coin.

"Mr. Morgan! Come on in!" he beckoned, before closing his book and setting it to the side of his desk to clear the space in front of him.

Then he reached into one of the drawers and retrieved the copy of my manuscript I had shared with him. The front page was littered with markings and notes in the margin. I took a deep breath, trying not to take it personally. It was the first draft after all, and Professor Campbell was a published author, so he knew what the agencies would be looking for.

"Now don't get too worried," he quickly assured me, holding out his hands placatingly. Was I that transparent? "A lot of my notes are compliments or questions I had along the way that I know you'll be able to answer once you go back through."

I could only nod at first, still taking deep breaths in hopes of getting rid of that little knot behind my sternum. He began to flip through the pages, pausing only to adjust his spectacles.

"You said you were conducting interviews, correct?"

"Yes." I bent down to grab my interview questions from my bag and then placed them on the desk. "I'm going to interview my father when I go home for Christmas. I've also gotten the phone number of a woman who served as an army nurse."

He hummed thoughtfully. "That sounds great, but can you not speak to the woman in person? I find in-person interviews to be preferable. You can see the emotions of the person and hear them better, too."

I didn't know where Ellen's family lived. I could only assume it wasn't Edinburgh since she didn't share an address with me.

"I'd have to see where she's located, but maybe I

can make it work over winter break," I offered.

We then directed our attention back to the manuscript, focusing on the edits that had more of an impact on the story itself. While I had originally taken the markings to heart, I was now completely open to any and all suggestions and criticisms he had. This would—hopefully—be my first publication, and I wanted to enter the literature world as an author on a good foot. A great foot, even.

"Overall, Mr. Morgan, this is a wonderful piece," he smiled at me. "Once you get those firsthand stories, you'll be able to truly breathe life into it; capture the raw emotions of the time and put the reader right there in the midst of it all."

"That's the goal."

"I know you can accomplish it."

The muscles in my shoulders loosened at his encouragement. I felt more confident in my work than I had in a while.

"I really appreciate your help, Professor. Truly," I thanked him as I packed up my things, taking the edited manuscript with me.

"I'm keen to see what you come up with over the break."

My break. Right. It wasn't going to be much of a

break.

As I walked home, I mentally went through my schedule. This time of year was, of course, one of the busiest times at the bookshop, so Mr. Graham had me scheduled during the week as well. Thankfully, he'd decided to close the shop on Christmas Eve and Day.

I'd need to speak to Ellen's mother right away and figure out if interviewing her in person would even be an option. Then I'd have to determine how long it would take to get to her and back.

By the time I reached my house, I had quite the headache. A solid cup of peppermint tea was in order. While the kettle boiled on the stove top, I retrieved the slip of paper Ellen had given me from under the sugar jar, having tucked it there so I wouldn't lose it. My room was currently a mess of papers between final exams and my book. The small scrap would have been lost within seconds, and I had the feeling Ellen wouldn't be too pleased if I had to bother her again for the number.

The kettle let out a screech, just as demanding as the woman I was thinking of, and the pain in my head sharpened. I quickly removed the kettle and poured the boiling water into my mug. Right away, I could smell the peppermint and that alone soothed the aching some. It had barely cooled before I took a drink. The steaming liquid burned down my throat, and then the warmth spread through my chest and belly. I sipped the tea, waiting for the headache to abate before I called Mrs. McLean.

When I'd finished and the throbbing had turned to a dull ache, I set down my empty cup and took up the receiver. Keeping it pressed to my ear with my shoulder, I held the number in one hand and dialed with the other.

It seemed to only ring a handful of times before a cheerful voice answered. "McLeans. How can I help ye?"

"Hello, Mrs. McLean," I greeted. "This is Fergus Morgan. I believe your daughter spoke to ye about me interviewing you for my book?"

"Oh aye!" I could hear the smile in her voice. So far, she was nothing like her daughter. "Ye wanted to ken about my time as an army nurse, correct?"

"Aye, ma'am." I fiddled with the phone cord, twisting it around my hand and then tugging gently. "If ye dinna mind, I'd like to do it in person. Winter holiday will be starting soon if ye'd be available."

I held my breath, but I wasn't sure which

outcome I wanted the most: cram a visit with her into my schedule or make do with an interview over the phone.

"That sounds nice, but I'm no so sure ye want to be spending your time off trekking into the Highlands. We're all the way up here in Beauly, outside of Inverness."

My mind did a quick calculation of the trip. It'd be just under four hours to get to Inverness by train and then a half-hour to Beauly. Giving the interview a generous estimate of a couple hours, I would then have a half-hour drive back to Inverness to catch the train home, arriving for a late supper. That is, of course, if the weather cooperated. Hard to tell in the winter, and especially traveling into the Highlands.

At most, it would take a little over a day. Giving up a free day with no obligations was worth it to me. My book needed not only the perspective of the soldiers, but also the nurses who served alongside them.

"That's no problem at all, Mrs. McLean," I insisted.

"Aye, well, I cannae expect ye to come all this way for only a day. We've got extra room now that all the laddies have moved out. And I'm sure Ellen would be more than happy to show ye around our little village or take ye into Inverness. In fact, the two of ye could ride the train together."

I could hardly respond to her; my mouth had gone dry, and my mind blank. Travel to the Highlands with Ellen? And then stay at her *house*? It was a recipe for disaster. We had managed to be civil the one night I'd walked her home in the rain, but even then, she'd snipped at me enough times to assure me we were barely even acquaintances.

I was going to need another cup of tea. Or two.

"Aye. Let me look at my schedule and see if that will work, but I really don't mind coming for just a day."

"If it doesna work, I understand. Either way, ken the offer is there should ye get here and change your mind," she assured me. "Even if it's just for the night."

That at least seemed manageable. One night and then I could be fresh for the train back to Edinburgh. It'd also give me a solid four hours to write without the distraction of my siblings or parents.

"I will. Thank ye again, Mrs. McLean, for letting me interview ye. Let alone welcoming me into your home."

"Thank ye for asking, Fergus. I look forward to meeting ye."

I bid her goodbye and then hung up, slumping forward until my forehead lightly thumped against the wall. Times like these made me wonder why I even bothered with a schedule if I would just have to redo it over and over again.

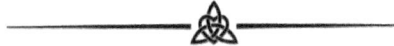

The sight of Ellen at my table gave me mixed feelings. While I wasn't exactly looking forward to her reaction when I told her I would be joining her on her trip home for the holidays, I was glad she was here so I could get the miserable experience over with as soon as possible. Then I could avoid her and the thought of it until the end of the semester.

I figured my presence next to her would be enough to get her attention, but she continued to scribble in her notebook, so I cleared my throat. Nothing. Pressing my lips together tightly, I did my best to keep calm. I needed to make sure my voice was as kind as possible once I actually spoke. I didn't want to get her hackles up right from the start. She had a short fuse even on a good day.

Before I could open my mouth to speak, she deliberately set down her pen and then turned to me, giving me a smile that was clearly forced, the edges of her mouth tense.

"Yes, Fergus."

Here goes nothing.

"I spoke to your mother about interviewing her in person, and she invited me to join ye as ye travel home," I shared.

The "smile" completely vanished, and she just stared at me blankly for a couple beats. I couldn't recall a time Ellen had been at a loss for words.

"Excuse me?" she finally managed, her voice barely more than a squeak.

I held back a sigh. I really didn't want to say it the first time, and I still hadn't even gotten to the worst part. "Your mother invited me to travel to Beauly with ye so I can interview her in person. She offered for me to stay the night to make the trip worth my time, but–"

"*What?*"

Now her eyes were practically bugging out of her head. Her chest rose and fell at an unnaturally rapid pace, and her hands had tightened into fists. I had half a mind to move away in case one of those fists came my way. I wouldn't put it past her. But then she stood, the wooden legs of her chair scraping harshly across the floor, and began to pace back and forth in front of the shelves. A couple students passing by paused to ogle us, and the last thing I needed was them drawing more attention and alerting the librarian.

"Ellen." I stepped forward cautiously.

She ignored me, so the next time she came close enough, I reached out to gently grasp her arm. Her body shook under my hand.

"Ellen. Please sit," I urged her.

Her eyes met mine, and the waves of the loch were choppy. She was panicking. Now I was even more determined to get her back in her seat and calmed down. Thankfully, she took little prodding, resuming her spot from before, but her body remained rigid.

"Deep breaths," I encouraged, letting my hand drop.

"I ken what to do," she snapped.

Well, at least she was well enough to yell at me. I claimed the seat next to her, but made sure to give her space. There was nothing worse than being crowded when you were feeling overwhelmed.

"I'd say that I dinna have to come if it makes ye uncomfortable, but I really do need to speak to your mother in person. I can get a hotel room in Inverness if I need to. And I willna be in your home more than is necessary," I tried.

She shook her head. "It's fine. I–I'm just overwhelmed at the moment."

I took in the mess in front of her. She'd never kept a tidy workspace, but today it looked as if her things had exploded on the table. There were papers and books scattered everywhere, the floor included, and I spotted what must have been the rough draft of her essay—before she scribbled the poor thing to death—peeking out from under a pile of tomes.

"The essay for your professor, I assume?"

Her jaw tightened, and she nodded.

Before I could stop myself, I held out my hand. "Here. Let me see what ye have."

She eyed me skeptically. "Ye don't ken anything about biomedical sciences."

A snide remark was on the tip of my tongue, but she wasn't wrong. Science had never been my forte; the equations were difficult to memorize, and the concepts too abstract. Even if words were my specialty, scientific terminology often went over my head.

"Aye, but I ken a lot about writing and writing well."

Surprisingly, she dug out what she had and slid it over to me. There were several pages, so I made myself comfortable, sinking down into the chair as I read them over. Ellen was quiet beside me, but the nerves were still radiating off of her.

"First thing, ye've repeated this one idea four times." I pointed to the area I was referencing when she leaned over for a better look.

For a second time, the distinct, floral scent of her perfume enveloped me. I still couldn't place the exact flower.

"Oh. I didna even realize I did that," she mused, bringing my focus back to the paper.

I quickly skimmed the rest of it, but it was much harder with her peering over my shoulder.

"Overall, I think ye've got a solid idea here, it just needs better organization."

I sat up and was relieved whenever she did the same, sufficiently backing out of my personal space. She snorted; the table in front of us was evidence enough that organization was not exactly Ellen's strong suit.

"Would ye mind if I took this with me to look over? I've got a typewriter at home and could whip up a new draft for ye with a better structure by tomorrow," I offered without a second thought.

Then ye can at least read the godforsaken thing. I kept that thought to myself.

"Are ye sure?" Ellen asked hesitantly.

"It'd be my way of making it up to ye for intruding on your trip home." It was the least I could do. "And there's no way I can—in good conscience—allow ye to turn this mess in. The point is to get a better grade, is it no?"

Her eyes rolled at that, and I was actually glad to see the expression. This was the Ellen I'd grown accustomed to. I knew how to respond to this Ellen.

"Och, dinna think so highly of yourself," she scoffed, shoving away from me to return to her books. "And here I was beginning to think ye weren't as much of a pompous arse as I originally thought. Apparently even *I* can be wrong sometimes."

Chapter 6

Ellen

December

I'd been bumped into without so much as an apology or acknowledgement of any kind more times than I'd faced down one of Fergus' scowls. So much for holiday spirit and spreading cheer. I felt like a Scrooge more and more by the minute.

One thing that did make me fairly cheerful, though, was the fact I had yet to see Fergus. Our train left in just ten minutes, and as I stood amongst the masses, I entertained myself with possible reasons for his absence—one of which may have involved *minor* bodily harm. All of them, of course, ended with him not coming at all.

My mood only improved as time went on. The train arrived and I joined a queue to load onto one of the cars. A quick glance left and right showed no sign of the dark head of hair I dreaded so much. Maybe this would be a joyful holiday after all.

When I'd offered for Fergus to interview my mother, I hadn't figured it would be in person, let alone require him to tag along on my trip home for Christmas. The holidays were meant to be spent with family. Not the friend of a friend who was sometimes decent to you, but more often than not, plotting your demise because you sat at a damn table.

Could I have just found a different table? Absolutely. But it was the principle of the thing. The table didn't belong to anyone, and I had just as much right to sit there as he did.

If I were being honest with myself, my discomfort with him coming to my childhood home wasn't because of his obsession with that stupid table. An admittedly attractive male would be coming home with me for the holidays. It'd happened only once before, and I had vowed never again to welcome a man into my safe place.

A not-so-subtle nudge from behind brought my

attention back to the present. I lifted my skirt slightly so as not to step on the thick wool as I ascended the metal stairs and followed the gentleman in front of me through the doorway. The first rows of seating were already claimed. I leaned around the gentleman to look for an empty seat, only for my stomach to drop and the blood to drain from my face.

Fergus was fairly tall, so he sat high enough I could confirm it was him and not some other dark-haired bloke. He had yet to spot me, his nose already buried in a book, so I spun on my heel and started swimming upstream to get to the next car, much to the annoyance of the other passengers behind me. I placed my suitcase in front of me as a deterrent, and the going was smoother as people ducked out of my way.

There was just one seat left in the next car and I quickly claimed it, heaving out a breath as I sank into the lumpy cushion. This was happening then. Fergus would be in my home. The one place in the entire world I could be completely myself with no fear of judgement or ridicule.

The train pulled away from the station, and I decided a distraction was best; it wasn't worth spending the entire trip fretting over what would happen when we got there. I retrieved a book from my suitcase and happily disappeared into the intriguing world of human anatomy. I only came up for air when the ticket collector came through the car and again when my stomach growled loud enough for the man across the aisle from me to shoot me a look. Thankfully, I'd packed a snack to tide me over.

By the time we arrived at Inverness, I'd filled more than three pages of my notepad with my thoughts and important bits of the book I wanted to remember. I would have to finish it later tonight after supper.

My thoughts then went to the unwanted guest that would be joining us at the dining table. I still could not believe my mother had invited him to stay. Having him visit was one thing, but actually sleeping under the same roof was a different thing entirely. There would be no reprieve. I'd have to continue masking, lest I give him new reasons to taunt me.

If anything, it was the thought of my mother's cooking that got me up and moving. I may have been frustrated with her, but I could never say no to her bannocks and homemade jam. With everything back in my suitcase and the clasps secure, I followed the other passengers off the train and onto the platform.

The Beauly station wasn't nearly as busy as Edinburgh's had been, but there was still a good amount of foot traffic for the small village. I took a moment to breathe in the fresh Highland air. It felt good to be back amongst the snow-capped mountains and fields dotted with sheep. While the people of Edinburgh were a bit more open-minded than the stubborn Highlanders, it was still home, and I'd always have a soft spot for it in my heart.

I turned to see Fergus making his way towards me. Suppose I'd have to play gracious host until I could pawn him off on my father.

I tilted my head towards the end of the platform closest to the ticket booth. "Da said he'd meet us over there. Ye'll probably be able to see him before me, being the giant that ye are, so look for a man with unkempt, gray hair and a thick pair of spectacles. Makes him look like an owl."

He chuckled to himself, "Sounds like Professor Campbell."

I didn't know who Professor Campbell was, and I didn't care to know more about the man, so I started towards the ticket booth, leaving Fergus to follow me or get lost. Wouldn't that be a lovely idea?

But alas, he stuck close with his long strides, not letting anyone walk between us.

"I think I see him."

Sure enough, I caught a glimpse of my father between the moving bodies. Just before we got to him, the crowd thinned out enough that he saw me and waved eagerly, his blue eyes sparkling.

"Ellen!" The second I was within reach, he pulled me tight into his embrace. "It's good to have ye home, dearie."

I wrapped my free arm around him in return and buried my face into his wool coat, breathing in his signature scent; pine with a touch of cigar. It reminded me of sitting on his lap after supper and listening to the radio programs as a child. It was the only time I truly got him to myself and didn't have to share his attention with my brothers.

He pulled back, breaking my moment of nostalgia.

"Da, this is Fergus..." I hesitated and glanced back at him, unsure of his last name. I didn't think I'd ever heard it, in fact.

"Morgan," he supplied, reaching out his hand. "Fergus Morgan. Thank ye again for hosting me."

Da just smiled brightly back at him and shook his

hand. "Of course. I ken my wife is verra excited to talk to ye about her time in the war."

A certain emotion flicked across his face, but it was gone before I could fully decipher it. While Mam would happily talk about her experiences all day if she could, Da would rather not dwell on memories of the war. He had initially avoided being drafted due to his impaired vision. By the time they had revised their vision standards, Da was the sole caretaker of my brothers and me as Mam had gone to the front lines.

"In fact,"—Da's eyes turned to me—"she'll be nagging at me if I dinna get ye home as soon as possible. She's been cooking all day, saying ye need a proper meal for once."

I scoffed, the sound coming from the back of my throat. "Och. Does she no think I can cook?"

Da just shrugged his shoulders up to his ears and raised his hands in defense. He'd never choose sides between Mam and me when we were having a row. Even my brothers, who were always ready for a fight, would hightail it out of the house the second we started going at each other. To say we butted heads when I was growing up was an understatement.

"I'm parked this way," Da cocked his head in the

direction of the street.

He reached out to take my suitcase from me and then offered his arm. I obliged and tucked my hand into the crook of his elbow, nice and cozy pressed against his side. Had any other man tried it, I would have asserted that I was perfectly capable of carrying the suitcase myself, but this was my father, and I knew he would've done the same for any of my brothers. He always tried to make others' lives easier.

He insisted on taking Fergus' suitcase as well once we got to the car and loaded it into the boot while Fergus climbed into the passenger seat. I slid into the back with a frown, a little miffed to have my spot taken. The twitch of Fergus' mouth told me he noticed. Prick.

Da barely had time to put the car in park before I'd opened my door. I beelined to the front door, which was unlocked like always.

"Mam?!"

I knew she was in the kitchen before she even called out to tell me so. The most mouth-watering aroma wafted from that direction, and I followed it like a hunting dog tracking their prey. However, at the end of my trail was my mother slaving over several pots on the stove.

She'd messily piled her greying, brown hair on top of her head, the nest desperately pinned to keep the wayward locks out of her face. The kitchen was sweltering, prompting her to open the window above the sink to let in the cold air. She turned at the sound of my footsteps, and her face lit up much like Da's had. Suppose it had been a while since I'd been home.

"Oh, Ellen," she cooed, pulling me in for a tight hug.

"Hi, Mam."

The hug only lasted a few more seconds before she pulled back, hands still on my arms, and peered around me. "Where on earth is the lad?"

As if on cue, the two men came stamping in the door, Da shutting it tight behind them. While the kitchen may have been a sauna from all the cooking, the rest of the house tended to stay chilly from multiple drafts in the old cottage. By the time they reached the kitchen, they had already shed their coats, unlike me.

"Oh, *mo ghraidh*," Da sighed as he walked over to the stove for a peek. "I think ye've outdone yourself."

Mam smiled affectionately before nudging him away before he could try to sample anything.

"Fin and Blair are coming for supper. Callum willna be here 'til Christmas. Work's keepin' him." Her attention then turned to Fergus, standing awkwardly in the doorway. "And we have our guest here who I believe deserves a proper Highland supper as a welcome."

She reached him within two steps and wrapped her arms around him, Fergus easily dwarfing her. For a moment, he looked a bit shocked and unsure, but then he hugged her back.

"Thank ye again for having me. Sounds like ye've already got a full house."

Mam flicked her hand dismissively through the air as she backed away and returned to the stove. "Nothing I'm no used to."

"If anything, she doesna ken how to cook for any less than six people," Da chimed in, teasingly patting his stomach. "Not that I mind."

Mam scoffed affectionately before glancing over her shoulder at me. "Ellen. Why don't ye show Fergus to the boys' old room so he can get settled?"

The boys' room. Right across from mine.

If he actually stays the night, I reminded myself.

I needed to take my suitcase up to my own room, so I motioned for Fergus to follow me, pausing in the foyer long enough to get our things.

"Watch the second step," I warned as we approached the old stairs. "There's a dent where my brother, Callum, hit his head."

Chapter 7

Fergus

There was, in fact, a decent dip in the step, and I carefully bypassed it, grateful for my long legs. Despite her much shorter legs, Ellen had already made it halfway up the stairs. I took them two at a time, catching up to her just as she reached the top.

Her eyes widened when she turned to find me right there, and she took a step away before nodding towards one of the three doors in the short hallway.

"That's the lads' room there," she stated.

Then she opened the door to our right, stepped in, and promptly shut it behind her. Not that I wanted to stand there and chat anyway. I was eager to get my things and return to the kitchen to speak with Mrs. McLean.

I'd heard three different names mentioned, and I tried to imagine three teenage boys fitting into a room this size. There was only one bed now, and I set my suitcase on it so I could retrieve the list of questions I'd typed up and my notepad. I tucked a few extra pens into my pocket, should one give out on me. I didn't have the luxury of a recorder, so I would have to rely on my note-taking skills to capture everything I needed.

When I returned to the kitchen, Mr. McLean had joined his wife at the stove, stirring something in a giant pot. The sight of them working on dinner together surprised me, given my mother would have never let my da anywhere near the kitchen.

The old wood floors creaked beneath me, signaling my arrival.

"Just a moment, dear, and I'll be right with ye. We can sit at the table," Mrs. McLean addressed me.

"Of course."

I sat down so I could organize my things before she joined me, laying my questions next to my notepad and placing all the pens on the table for easy access. Wiping her hands on her apron, Mrs. McLean left the managing of the food to her husband

and sat across from me with an expectant and open expression. While there were gray streaks through her hair, I could still see the rich brown underneath, just a touch lighter than Ellen's hair. They had the same nose, though. Petite and perky like the nose of the faeries in my childhood storybooks.

I refocused my attention on my list of questions. "What made ye want to become a nurse?"

"I'd taken care of my father after he lost his leg in the first war. He took a bullet to the shin, but there weren't enough medics and his injury was deemed less urgent. Gas gangrene took over quickly and he ended up losing his leg up to his mid-thigh. His quality of life could have been different had he received the help he needed." She nodded resolutely, "If I could save a man from my father's fate, then I'd have served my purpose here on Earth."

There was only the sound of my pen scratching across the paper and the gentle scrape of a wooden spoon on the inside of a pot. I looked up at Mrs. McLean once more. "And how did ye go from caring for your father to being an army nurse?"

"I started my nursing career training at Muirfield Hospital in Inverness. They serviced the poor and elderly and were in desperate need of staff. I found it fulfilling helping those who couldna afford the highest quality services.

"I'd just finished training when I became pregnant with Callum and had to leave the hospital. Blair followed just two years later, and Finlay after that. They kept me just as busy as my patients ever had, but it wasna the same. Bandaging scraped knees wasna quite as thrilling as assisting a doctor with a life-saving procedure," she smiled ruefully.

The curve of her lips flattened then, and she adjusted in her seat. "Then the war broke out in thirty-nine as ye ken. Several of the young men here in Beauly went off to fight."

Mrs. McLean glanced out the window above the sink, her eyes far away as if she were seeing something that wasn't there. I just saw a field with woolly sheep scattered about.

"Not even a year in, Mrs. Stewart lost her husband. An explosive went off close enough to him that the pressure waves caused a concussion. Medics didna recognize the signs of intracranial bleeding until it was too late." Her eyes returned to me, confident and controlled once more. "It was then I kent I needed to go."

"And what was Mr. McLean's opinion on the

matter?" I asked curiously, glancing towards the man at the stove. His back faced us, but I could see the tension in his neck.

"He wasna happy about it. I dinna ken a soul who would happily send their spouse off to war. But he also kent the woman he married."

I swore I heard a low chortle from Mr. McLean.

Her mouth twisted in an expression I'd seen Ellen wear a handful of times. "It wasna a decision we came to in one sitting. Nor did we take it lightly. It wasna just us we had to consider, after all. Wee Finlay had just turned one. Taking care of a child on your own can be arduous, let alone three rowdy boys under the age of five. It was a lot to ask of my husband and I cannae tell ye how many nights I spent crying at the idea of leaving him and the bairns in such uncertain times."

She fiddled with a dishcloth in her hands, eyes locked on the fabric twisting and looping through her fingers. My pen glided across the paper as fast as my hand could go, but I did my best to keep my eyes on Mrs. McLean so she knew I was genuinely listening. Her story wasn't one made up for a book. She and her husband had lived it.

"We spent nearly a year going back and forth on

the matter. Then I found out I was pregnant with Ellen, and we were back to square one." She laughed and shook her head. "Here I'd thought I was too old to carry any more bairns, but Ellen proved me wrong."

I laughed as well. "Sounds like her."

Mrs. McLean smiled before continuing. "So, I waited to enlist until forty-two, once wee Ellen was old enough to wean and make do without her mother. Then I returned home in forty-five when the war ended."

I tried to imagine my mother leaving when any of my siblings or I were so young. My father had missed most of my mother's pregnancy with me and didn't return until I was almost two, but it was different for a father than for a mother. Plenty of men went off to war and left their wives pregnant or caring for several young children. However, it felt unheard of for a mother to leave her bairns so young to be minded by their father.

"Was it hard for ye, leaving your family?" I asked without thinking whether that was an appropriate question to ask or not; I was too curious.

"Aye. I kent well how important those first years are with your bairns. And here I had my first girl. But what would I be teaching my children if I didna help when I had the means to?"

I flipped to a fresh new page before asking my next question.

"I'd like to ask about your time in the war now. Ye can share whatever you're able to and feel comfortable with," I assured her.

She seemed to steel herself, adjusting in her seat so she sat straight as a rod. I held my pen at the ready.

"Suppose I'll start with the positives first and slowly ease into the rest. Most people dinna think there can be pockets of joy during a war, but we made them when we could." The corner of her lips twitched up in a hint of a smile. "One soldier was a talented artist, and he'd leave little sketches of people around the base. I still have mine. The paper's worn and tattered, but ye can still see the drawing clear as day."

Soldiers and nurses were the same as anyone else with careers, hobbies, and talents. I made a note to myself to add examples in my story to make the characters more relatable by revealing bits of who they were outside of the war.

"Then there was Johnny. He was sweet on one of

the nurses, and I swear he was in the med tent every single day."

I raised a brow curiously with an amused smile. "I take it he didna really need any medical attention?"

"Och, no. He'd always come up with some excuse or another. Blurry vision, a migraine, or something else easily treatable. But if Elizabeth wasna on duty, his ailments magically cured themselves." Her smile faltered. "'Til the day he came in with a piece of shrapnel in his eye."

I winced, my own eye aching just at the thought of it.

"He told Elizabeth she was the most beautiful girl he'd ever seen, and now she always would be. I dinna ken what happened to them, as I was sent off to Normandy soon after. But I'd like to think they both made it home and got married."

She continued to talk about the injuries she'd seen and treated, such as the time she'd assisted with a facial reconstruction. There'd been significant medical advancements since the First World War, but the weapons had also grown more advanced.

Ellen's father made each of us a cup of tea, and I accepted it gratefully. Mrs. McLean spoke in such a way that you felt as if you were right there beside her experiencing it all. I needed to be reminded I was in a cottage kitchen in the Scottish Highlands and years away from that horrific war.

Clearly, Professor Campbell had been correct about an in-person interview being better. I'd completely filled pages upon pages with as much of her words as I could capture, even noting her vocal or facial expressions when I could, whether it be a laugh and a reverent smile or a more haunted look as if she were seeing the injured and dead at that very moment, laid out on the table between us.

"I believe that's all, Mrs. McLean. I cannae tell ye how much I appreciate ye sharing this with me."

She gave me a gentle smile. "Thank ye for listening to me. It's nice to acknowledge those who were there with me. They deserve to be remembered."

Chapter 8

Fergus

The Highland air was brisk and had a bite to it when I stepped outside, pulling my scarf tighter around my neck to keep the chill from creeping down my back. I needed some time to process what Mrs. McLean had shared and also figure out how I would use it for my book, but I didn't feel like being cooped up in the spare room to do so.

Supper would be at six, so I'd have time to explore the quaint village of Beauly, seeing as how I'd most likely never be here again. I made pit stops along the way to visit the livestock, in no hurry. A few curious sheep allowed me to pat their woolly heads and scratch their chins, but the Highland coos a few fields down the dirt road couldn't care less about my presence. Not a single car passed me as I meandered towards the center of the village.

The dry-stone walls gave way, and the houses snuggled close together the further I walked. Turning onto High Street, the main road of the village, I spotted the church ruins Mr. McLean had mentioned looming up at the end of the street, surrounded by headstones and trees that had shed their foliage many months ago. One in particular caught my eye due to its peculiar shape, the branches thick and gnarled.

Nearing the ruins, I recognized a familiar figure beneath the bare elm, nestled within its roots.

"I thought ye were still in your room," I called out.

Ellen looked up and then shrugged. "I snuck out while ye were talking to Mam."

From this vantage point underneath the tree, she had a beautiful view of the Beauly River winding its way through the village and back into the mountains.

"I cannae say I blame ye for sneaking off to a place like this," I mused.

"This is the Wych Elm." I looked down to find her

admiring the tree, hand pressed affectionately to the rough bark of its trunk. "It's the oldest elm tree in Europe; over seven hundred years old."

I was awestruck. The oldest elm in the entirety of Europe and it was here in this small Scottish village.

"Here." Ellen stood and brushed stray pieces of bark and grass from her skirt. "I'll show ye around the priory."

Her offer surprised me, but I wasn't about to question her kindness. Figuring Ellen would be able to tell me more about the history of the ruins than the plaques scattered throughout, I eagerly followed her through the gate and down the path. At this time of day, the sun was just behind what remained of the priory, shining through the three front windows in heavenly rays.

"Oh my," I breathed out.

A smile came to Ellen's face as she gazed up at the priory. I could count the number of times I'd seen her smile on one hand, but boy, was it a bonnie smile.

"It is quite beautiful, isn't it?" she mused. "The priory was established by a group of monks who settled here in 1230. But like most of the Highlands, it didna make it through the Reformation. The other buildings were looted, and the stones taken to build Cromwell's fort in Inverness. Only the church was left."

We stepped through the open doorway and carefully picked our way across the stones to avoid stepping on any of the graves. A handful of headstones stood guard throughout the hall. Neither of us spoke—the place seemed to call for silence and reverence—but we stayed close together as we explored. I paused more often than Ellen, trying to read what I could of the worn names on the headstones.

When I stopped outside of the north transept to look through the window at the tomb inside, Ellen joined me. Her shoulder momentarily pressed against mine as she leaned up on her toes to peek through as well. I instinctively went to place my hand on the small of her back to help brace her, but thankfully stopped myself just before I touched her. She was being surprisingly pleasant, and I wasn't about to ruin that. We still had to make it through tonight and tomorrow morning.

"It's the tomb of Sir Kenneth Mackenzie of Kintail," she explained, her voice quiet.

I'd somehow forgotten what I was looking at and

reverted my attention back to the tomb with the detailed effigy of the clan chieftain. Compared to the rest of the memorials, it was by far in the best condition, most likely due to it being protected by the wooden door.

I turned to share a fact I'd learned about Mackenzie from Doug and found myself staring into the depths of Ellen's deep blue irises, the words dying instantly on my lips. I remembered the first time I'd seen her eyes: dark pools of blue just brimming with anger and annoyance. That wasn't the case now. The last few rays of sunlight reflecting off of them reminded me of St. Margaret's Loch on a rare sunny day in Edinburgh, a refreshing blue you just wanted to dive headfirst into—no monsters lurking this time.

Voices chatting behind us and the sound of footsteps on stone caused us both to jerk back, glancing behind to see a group wandering into the priory.

"I-uh. I suppose we should get back," I stumbled for an excuse, rubbing my hand down the nape of my neck. "I dinna want to be an ungracious guest and show up late to supper."

"Right," she agreed. "Cannae have ye panicking

on me because ye were late for once."

The taunt fell flatter than usual, her heart seemingly not in it at the moment.

We waited long enough for the group to pass us and then picked our way back to the exit. Returning down the road to her house, there were fewer livestock out; most likely having found a spot to nestle in for the night. The sheep were still near the dry-stone, though, and Ellen halted long enough to scratch the chin of one who had propped his feet on the stones to see us better.

"And here I thought I was special," I grumbled, eyeing the unfaithful buck. He let out a low bleat in response.

Ellen cocked an amused eyebrow at me over her shoulder. "Och, they're just giant puppy dogs. They'll take any attention they can get."

Accepting that the sheep hadn't been kind to me because I was a stranger, I stepped forward to scratch the buck behind his ears. His eyes closed in complete bliss. Then, with a shake of his head and one last parting bleat, he shoved off the wall and returned to the herd.

Ellen and I turned to continue down the road, and I tucked my hands into my pockets. While I was used to there being tension between the two of us, this felt different, and I couldn't quite place it.

"Oh." I turned my upper body slightly towards her. "I meant to ask how everything turned out with your essay."

Ellen's face brightened, and her chest puffed out proudly as she smiled at me. "Nearly perfect score. Honestly, I think the man was reaching for anything he could to mark me down even just a few points."

My heart swelled with pride, even if it wasn't mine to claim. Yes, I had helped with the structure of her essay, but Ellen was the one who'd created the content. They were her ingenious thoughts and ideas.

"I cannae thank ye enough, Fergus," she added earnestly.

I waved my hand dismissively. "Och. The score is all you. I just moved bits around and cleaned it up."

"Ye got my point across clearer than I ever could," she argued. "That's the one part I struggle with is getting all these thoughts in my head down on paper in a way others can understand what I mean."

"Well, I am happy to help ye with formatting any future assignments. Your thoughts deserve to be heard."

The flush of her cheeks could've easily been from the cold—Ellen wasn't one to be shy or embarrassed—but then she'd turned her head away before I could be sure.

When we reached the house, there was no time to think about it; before she even opened the door, I could hear voices from within. We had barely hung up our coats when two men crammed through the doorway from the family room.

"Corbie!" they cried in unison.

They were both fair-haired like their father, but they were clearly her brothers. They all had the same eyes. The tallest one scooped Ellen up into his arms and held her tight despite her protests. Given that her own arms were pinned to her sides, all she could do was kick him in the shins.

"Put me down, ye big oaf!" she barked out, "We get it. You're the tallest."

"And strongest," he grinned proudly.

The other brother's eyes were locked on me, and I ducked my head a bit, half-tempted to step back out the door.

"Corbie," he gasped, now looking at Ellen, who had been begrudgingly placed back down on the ground. "Did ye finally bring home a laddie?"

Her face turned crimson in record time. "He's not mine. He's an English major who wanted to interview Mam about her time in the war for his book."

I figured that was my cue to step in and confirm her explanation, so I held out my hand to the one closest to me first.

"Fergus Morgan. It's nice to meet ye both."

He smiled brightly at me as he firmly shook my hand. "I'm Finlay, but feel free to call me Fin." His head tipped to his brother beside him. "This gowk is Blair."

"Came to talk to Mam, eh? I'm sure she talked your ear off with all her tales."

I managed a light chuckle. "I enjoyed every minute. It'll do my book good to have her insight."

As if her ears were burning, Mrs. McLean's head popped out from the kitchen, and she waved us all in. "I didna spend all day slavin' over a hot stove to have it go cold while the lot of ye stand there bletherin'."

She returned to the kitchen and the three McLean siblings rolled their eyes simultaneously. Ellen led the way, and Fin gestured for me to follow, the two brothers bringing up the rear.

"As if Da would ever let food go cold," Blair muttered under his breath. "He'd eat it all himself before he let that happen."

I found myself chuckling along with Fin, knowing that I'd do the exact same. The house had smelled heavenly ever since we'd arrived, and I didn't know how I'd managed to even focus during my interview, what with the food cooking not even three feet away from me.

Once we stepped into the dining area, Mrs. McLean patted the seat next to her. "Right here, Fergus."

I quietly thanked her and slipped into the seat. She insisted on making my plate for me as I was a guest, giving me a healthy helping of every dish. The boys were right behind, piling their plates so full that all the food intermingled. My eye twitched at the sight, and I looked down at my own plate, using my fork to nudge my tatties away from the juice creeping out from under the salmon.

Mrs. McLean had sat me right across from Ellen, and I couldn't decide if that was better or worse than having her sit right next to me. The issue with this positioning was how easily I randomly locked eyes with her. Thankfully, she was just as uncomfortable and would avert her gaze instantly. It seemed best to keep my eyes on my plate unless someone spoke to me directly, and given the fact that it most likely wouldn't be Ellen, I was safe in at least looking at who I was speaking to. Currently, that was Blair between his mouthfuls of food.

"Earlier, the two of ye called Ellen, Corbie. Why on earth do ye call her a crow?"

"Ah," he smiled, taking a peek over at his sister, who was having a fairly heated debate with Fin. "She collects things like a crow. As kids, we'd go out to play, and she'd always find the most unusual items, her favorites being animal bones. She knew exactly which part of the animal it was."

He shuddered dramatically and chuckled at himself for it, but I knew the feeling. Passing her in the library, I often saw the detailed medical drawings that always sent a shiver down my spine. Good to know she had upgraded from animals to human beings.

"Add on that she's the only one of us with dark hair. Seeing it flying behind her as she scampered through the fields reminded ye of a crow's wings."

I caught myself glancing over to said girl while

she was distracted by Fin. While her mother had light brown hair, Ellen's was much darker, and I wondered where it came from. Clearly not her father's side of the family.

"Ellen, did ye ever get that assignment sorted with your professor?" her father asked, sufficiently breaking up the bickering siblings.

"What happened with your professor?" Fin asked curiously.

Ellen let out a huff at the reminder of the situation. I, myself, remembered how upset she'd been that night at the library and what she'd shared with me about her professor. I couldn't believe he'd spoken to a student in such a way, female or male.

"He told me the topic I'd chosen was too advanced for me and heavily hinted that his opinion was due to my being a woman."

Fin smiled wryly. "And surely ye proved him wrong, aye?"

Ellen's expression shifted, and her smirk mirrored her brother's, making them look more alike than I'd originally thought. "I nearly got a perfect score on it. I wish I could've seen the look on his face when he read it."

"I will say, your daughter's passion for her work

is very inspiring."

I only realized I'd spoken aloud once the words had already fallen out of my mouth. Ellen looked at me with wide, surprised eyes, and I wished I could shovel them back in.

"Well, I'd say you're very passionate about your work as well, Fergus," Mrs. McLean replied. "What with your book and all."

"Aye, but it doesna spark a fire in my belly like the one I see in Ellen."

Now I had all the eyes of the McLean clan on me, and my cheeks flushed under the attention, but I was already in too deep. I had no choice but to trudge on.

"I care too much about others' opinions and making my book exactly what editors and publishing companies want. Ellen doesn't. She's exactly who she is, and everyone else can get on board or get out of her way." My gaze locked on Ellen. "It's very admirable, the confidence she has in herself."

"Well, that sounds like our lass for sure," Mr. McLean chuckled. "She's always been a very determined little thing."

"Och, you're telling me!" Fin scoffed before launching into a memory of Ellen when they were younger.

I was grateful for the attention being diverted to him, the rest of the family chiming in with their own memories of the story, but I could still feel Ellen's gaze boring into me. I took a sip of my water to wash down my last bite and then quietly excused myself to Mrs. McLean. She nodded distractedly, only giving me half her attention, and I doubted anyone else noticed as I left the room.

There weren't exactly many places for me to go in the small cottage, so I grabbed my coat and stepped outside. The Highland air had calmed and refreshed me earlier; surely it could help me wrap my mind around why I'd blurted that out about Ellen. The sun had set long ago, and my breath puffed out in a white cloud against the dark sky as I let out a deep sigh.

Then the door swung open behind me, the chatter of the McLeans loud for a split second before the door closed and muffled them again. I turned to find Ellen standing on the stoop with her eyebrows pinched together.

"What on earth was that?" she asked, a bit demanding. "Why did ye say all those things?"

My body heated instantly, and I frowned back at her, suddenly defensive. At least that was a feeling I understood. Especially when it came to Ellen.

"I was being polite, Ellen. Ye ken what politeness is, don't ye? What it is to be kind and pay someone a compliment?" I snapped back.

Now she was the one who didn't know what to say. She just stood there, glaring at me, and I glared back. Was she seriously mad at me for saying nice things about her to her family?

"Did ye mean it?" she asked finally.

There was a vulnerability in her voice, and the crease between her eyebrows had relaxed, the dark brows now arching upward in the middle curiously. I could easily lie to her and say no, throw back up the walls we'd slowly been picking at stone by stone. But that look on her face tugged at my heart, and I didn't want to hurt her. I had been completely honest in there, the words spilling out without a thought, because they were the truth. It was how I really felt.

"Aye, of course. I wouldna say it if I didna mean it," I assured her, my own voice soft like hers had been. "I'm sorry if I embarrassed ye. That was not my intention."

She tugged down on the sleeves of her sweater, and only then did I register that she had followed me out without a coat. I would've offered my own had I not expected her to refuse.

"Well, thank ye. Suppose I didna realize ye noticed so much about me."

"You're a rare woman, Ellen." I shrugged, "And when ye keep showing up everywhere I go, it's hard not to notice ye."

Chapter 9

Ellen

Blair had insisted we go out to the pub after supper for drinks. The local band was playing tonight, and all the bodies shoved into the already cramped space made the pub absolutely stifling. Fin had somehow managed to find us a table to crowd around and then flag down a waitress to order a round of pints. Thankfully, I'd found myself sandwiched between my brothers, with Fergus on the other side of Blair. I didn't think I could handle being so close to him at the moment.

I wasn't supposed to like Fergus Morgan. He was an extremely particular and annoyingly organized man who drove me insane more often than not. But then he'd said those things about me at supper, praising me for my determination and inability to back down from a challenge. Traits that were often looked down upon in women, he admired me for. Every time I thought about it, I felt my body flush with warmth, which was definitely a new feeling when it came to Fergus. Normally, he was making my face turn red with frustration, but now he had me genuinely blushing.

The second a pint was placed in front of me, I downed half of it. Blair cheered next to me and roughly bumped his shoulder into mine.

"That's our Corbie!" He threw back his own pint and gulped down every last drop before slamming the empty glass back onto the table. "One more pint and then I'm finding a bonnie lass to join me on the dance floor. You in, Morgan?"

My eyes involuntarily darted over to Fergus, who just laughed, raising his hands in compliance. "Alright, alright. I'm in."

There was a sharp stab in my chest, and I took another big drink to try and wash it away.

"I'm glad you're here to occupy him," Fin chuckled as Blair ambled off towards the bar. "Mari wouldna be happy if she heard I was dancing with some Beauly lass."

"Aye? And who's this Mari?" Fergus inquired.

My brother just grinned, looking absolutely love sick. "A beautiful Welsh lass I've been courtin' for a while now."

I blocked out the rest of their conversation, which wasn't too hard given the noise level of the pub. If people weren't out on the dance floor, they were crammed around the bar and tables just as we were, trying to be heard over the music. The band was admittedly good, though.

I thought I recognized the fiddler as someone I'd gone to secondary school with, and it took me a moment to place him. He had much more facial hair now than he had back then. A good number of my classmates had left Beauly and never came back. Still, there were a handful that had stayed and made a home for themselves here, like Blair had. I couldn't see myself returning to Beauly, no matter how much I adored the village. Edinburgh was far more my speed.

When Blair returned, he had two pints in each hand, apparently deciding we all needed another round. My glass was already three-quarters empty, so I appreciated his foresight. He barely let Fergus get down half of his own before Blair grasped his upper arm and dragged him away.

I watched over the rim of my pint as they approached two girls a couple tables over. Fergus stood a little behind Blair, letting him take the lead, but it was obvious he'd caught the attention of one of the lasses. Her eyes never left him once, and she all too eagerly led him to the dance floor once her friend had agreed to join my brother.

Within minutes, they were lost in the crowd, and the sting in my chest dulled once I couldn't see them anymore. When I turned to Fin, his attention was solely on me, and he had a knowing look on his face that I didn't like.

"So, when are ye finally gonna bring Mari to meet the family?" I asked before he could even say a word. "She's got to be houndin' ye by now. Ye've been together for how long?"

"Och. Only just over a year, but it wasna serious until the past few months. She'll meet all of ye soon enough," he waved his hand dismissively.

Fin was known to jump around from girl to girl, having probably courted every last one in Beauly by the time he left for Aberdeen. I think Mam was just glad to see him somewhat settling down, even if she hadn't met the lass who caused it yet.

"Have ye warned her about us?"

He laughed, a deep and throaty chuckle. "Aye, I have. Had to let her know what she was signing up for, eh?"

"And bless her heart for still stickin' with ye."

Our laughter dwindled, and we settled for enjoying our drinks, the music and surrounding chatter making it too difficult to have a proper conversation anyway. It wasn't long before I spotted Fergus again, and despite Fin sitting right next to me, I allowed myself to watch him. He was impressively light on his feet despite his height. Being so bookish, I hadn't expected him to be a very good dancer, but he was proving me wrong.

His hair had turned curly from working up a sweat, and I found it endearing; it gave him a boyish look much different from his usual slicked-back, put-together appearance. I wasn't the only one who noticed, though. It seemed the moment he finished a dance with one lass, another would appear. He danced with at least three. How many eligible women could be left in Beauly?

However, when the song ended, he bowed slightly to the girl he'd been with and dodged another as he made his way back to the table. He was breathing heavily and eagerly grabbed the nearest pint. I did my best not to stare as he tipped his head back to drain the glass.

"Aye, look at ye! I think Blair's upset ye've shown him up out there!" Fin laughed, holding his own pint out to Fergus in a cheers.

I wasn't sure if Fergus was blushing or if he was just flushed from the heat of the place and all the dancing. Then his eyes were on me, sparkling despite his clear exhaustion.

"Are ye not gonna dance?" he asked breathily.

"I'm no good. No lad would wanna dance with me unless he enjoyed having his toes stepped on."

He just tilted his head forward and gave me a look from under his thick lashes. "Och, come on. Ye cannae be so bad. Here. I'll dance with ye."

I instinctively shrank back even though I had nowhere to go, already pressed up against the corner of the booth. The last thing I wanted to do was embarrass myself in front of *him*. Then add on that two of my brothers were present, and I'd never hear the end of it.

"Ellen." His voice was more serious now.

I frowned at him. "Fergus."

He softened his features once more and held his hand out towards me across the table.

"Please," he asked gently.

It was no secret that the two of us were beyond stubborn and could have faced off all evening until last call, but I was honestly quite tired of constantly opposing him. So, with a deep breath to steady myself, I gave in and slid my hand into his. You would have thought I'd handed him a piece of gold with how brightly he beamed at me.

He led me towards the dance floor, keeping a tight hold of my hand as we wound through the other patrons. The dance floor was more cramped than I had realized watching from the outskirts, and I had no choice but to stand close to him whenever he found a spot he liked.

"Ready?" he asked, his pleased grin still in place as he turned to face me.

"No," I shook my head, but he just laughed.

Thankfully, he kept his steps simple so I could follow along—for the most part. We bumped into a few other dancers, but I didn't step on his toes once. That was a win in my book. Even better was that we'd missed the first half of the song, so we weren't dancing for very long.

The band transitioned easily into a slower song, and I moved to leave the dance floor, but Fergus' hold on my hand just tightened, and he tugged me back.

"I ken ye can dance to a slow song."

He raised his brows, just waiting for me to argue with him. Something about that look in his eyes kept me from it, and I found myself returning to him, only closer this time. There was that smile again as I moved my free hand to his shoulder, and his own found the small of my back. I realized I was holding my breath and tried to be discreet in letting it out.

"Your brothers are eyeing us," he murmured, amusement in his voice.

He gracefully turned us so I could look over at our table, where my brothers were in fact staring directly at us. Blair jokingly wiggled his brows, and I rolled my eyes back at him with a huff.

"Ye do realize ye've set me up to be teased and tormented the rest of the holiday, don't ye?" I eyed Fergus now, having to tilt my head back a bit to do so.

He at least had the decency to look apologetic. I let it slide and continued to sway back and forth with him, ignoring my brothers for now. Slow dancing wasn't really that bad, and, admittedly, neither was being this close to Fergus.

"Do ye have any siblings?" I asked suddenly.

Here he knew my family now—and clearly much more about me than I'd originally thought—and I knew nothing about him outside of academics.

"Aye," he affirmed, voice soft so as not to disrupt those around us. "An older brother, Euan, and my sister, Catriona, who is eight years younger than me. She was a bit of a surprise, but she's easily the favorite child."

"And you're not?" I gasped playfully.

He rolled his eyes, but smiled in amusement. "Suppose I was when it was just Euan and me. He was quite wild, so I did my best not to cause more trouble for my mam. Especially when Da was off at war."

I could relate to that. Bless my poor da, raising the four of us heathens alone for so long and all the while worrying about his wife. Surely, none of us had tried to make it any easier on him.

"Do ye remember your mam being gone?" he wondered.

I looked at him in slight shock. "Are ye a mind reader?"

He chuckled and shook his head. "She told me about leaving when ye were little during our interview."

"No. Not really," I admitted. "I dinna think anyone remembers much from the first few years of life, but I've heard enough stories from my brothers that I ken well enough what it was like."

"Do ye think it affected your relationship any?"

I pursed my lips. It wasn't exactly something I'd thought about. It was just how things were, and like I'd said, I didn't have very many memories from it.

"Possibly. I mean, I've always been closer with Da, but I dinna think it affected us too terribly. Sure, we fought during my adolescence, but who doesna butt heads with their parents at that age?"

"You're very much like her, ye ken. Neither of ye are gonna let a man tell ye what to do or anyone for that matter."

"I'm glad ye realize. Took you a bit, aye?" I raised a brow at him teasingly.

He made a deep noise in his throat that was a mix between amusement and irritation. He knew he couldn't argue with me on that one.

At some point, we'd wandered closer to each other. Fergus radiated heat and smelled of sweat and beer, but I didn't mind a bit. This time, it was Fergus who stepped away when the song ended, but his hands never left me, only moving from my back to my waist.

"Should I let the next lass in to dance with ye?" I teased. Surely there was another waiting.

"Och, no. I couldna do another song," he shook his head. "Besides, if they really knew me, I dinna think they'd be so interested. I'm sure they flock to any outsider who enters the pub."

He wasn't exactly wrong. Very few young people moved *into* Beauly, and it seemed like each year more and more left. Any stranger to the area drew attention, let alone one as handsome as Fergus and as talented a dancer.

"Honestly, I'm thinking I may head back. My train leaves early in the morning and I've never been able to fall asleep on a train."

"Right."

I stepped fully away from him now and turned towards our table. Both of my brothers were still there and, thankfully, no longer ogling the two of us. Instead, they looked deep in a conversation that proved to be an argument once Fergus and I got close enough.

"No, Callum told me that *you* were the one buying Da's gift."

Blair's face was red, and he stood at his full height, so he was glaring down at Fin. Knowing my brothers, something this simple could turn into a full-out brawl in two seconds. Without hesitation, I stepped between the two of them, even if I barely came up to Blair's armpit.

"Oi, ye two eejits. I bought Da's gift. Kent I couldna trust the lot of ye with that sort of responsibility."

"Oh."

The speed at which both of their bodies relaxed would've given anyone else whiplash. I, on the other hand, had spent my fair share of time with my brothers heavily inebriated.

"Thank ye, Corbie. Can always count on ye," Blair beamed, patting me on the head. He didn't even notice my glare, his attention now on Fergus. "Remind me to never take ye out again. The lassies clearly favor ye and I cannae be setting my ego up to be so damaged."

"Och," Fergus waved him off. "I'm just the shiny new toy."

He'd said if the lassies really knew him, they

wouldn't be interested, but I wasn't so sure about that. I never thought that I'd grow to tolerate the man, and yet here I was actually enjoying his company and conversation.

I had to be getting sick.

If I weren't, I surely would be soon. The stark contrast from the overheated pub to the bitter cold air outside was likely to send my body into shock. I clutched my coat tightly around me as Fin flagged down a cab for us.

The driver dropped my brothers off first at Blair's flat. Grateful for the extra room in the back, I didn't hesitate to slide over the second Fin had climbed out.

"See ye tomorrow, Corbie." I jumped back whenever he popped his head into the cab. "It was nice meetin' ye, Fergus. Don't let our little sister fool ye. She likes ye."

I quickly shoved his head back out of the vehicle, palm firmly placed over his mouth so he couldn't say anything else.

"Goodnight, Fin!"

I pulled the door shut the second he was clear of it, though at this point, I wouldn't really care if I'd caught a finger or two. Unbothered, the two of them just waved merrily at us until the cab driver took off.

I sat back in the seat with a sigh.

"They're a handful, aye?" Fergus chuckled next to me.

"You have no idea."

The drive home wasn't long at all. I pushed open the front door as quietly as possible, knowing the point at which the hinges would creak. We discarded our coats and boots in silence and padded towards the stairs. Despite a fair amount of alcohol in his system, Fergus remembered to avoid the second step.

I hesitated at my door, hand poised on the doorknob, and glanced back at Fergus. "If I dinna see ye before ye leave...I hope ye have a nice holiday with your family."

Even in the dark, I could see the corner of his lips quirk up.

"You, too. And thank ye for the dance."

I bowed my head in acknowledgement before slipping into my room and shutting the door behind me.

It was no secret I hadn't liked the idea of him coming to my home and infringing on my holiday. Yet somehow it had been a fairly enjoyable experience. At least this evening.

As I changed into my flannel pajamas and slipped under my heavy duvet, I wondered how this would affect us once we returned to Edinburgh. Would we actually be civil to each other, or would one of us crack the second the other did something that irritated them? If I were being honest with myself, I wasn't completely sure.

Chapter 10

Fergus

January 1962

I was relieved to be back at the bookshop, my refuge. While spending time with my family for Christmas had been great, I could only handle so much taunting and teasing from Euan. No one would ever guess he was the eldest.

Things had slowed, and I was happily spending my shift bringing order to the chaos left behind from holiday shopping. Currently, I was pulling all of the books that had been misplaced by careless customers, meticulously searching each and every shelf in the store. The pile on my cart had grown precarious, and I had to analyze where I placed each new addition like an architect, judging the weight and size of the book.

I had just finished the children's section—the worst of them all—when the bells chimed above the door and a blast of cold air swept through the shop.

"Hiya, Mr. Graham!"

I knew right away it was Doug; he was the only one stupid enough to greet the old man so cheerily. I looked over my shoulder to find him smiling brightly at the shop owner. Mr. Graham barely spared him a glance and just made some sort of grumbling noise that I assumed served as a response.

"I tell ye, he bloody loves me," Doug grinned as he strode towards me. "How'd ye like the Christmas gift I left ye?"

I paused my shelving to eye him, arms crossed over my chest. "Ye mean the Christmas card laid next to a sink full of dirty dishes?" I clarified.

He smiled sheepishly, shoulders creeping up towards his ears.

"Sorry about that. Freya wanted to bring a dish to Christmas supper, and we were running late. But ye saw the new ink for your typewriter, aye?"

"Aye, I did. Thank ye," I smiled gratefully,

causing his shoulders to relax once more.

I hadn't even told him I was running out. As scatter-brained as he could be at times, Doug was extremely thoughtful.

He stepped towards the tower of books and lifted the cover of the uppermost novel for a closer inspection, causing the stack to wobble dangerously. I reached out just in time to right it before any could topple off and then moved the cart a safe distance away from Doug.

Despite the fact that we'd both gone home to visit our families, who only lived a few streets apart, I hadn't seen him in over a week. He had stayed with his family longer—a much stronger man than I—so I'd had our place to myself the last few days. While I enjoyed the peace and quiet after being around my siblings, I still missed the presence of my best mate.

He pulled off his woolen hat and plopped down into a nearby chair. The stick straight blonde hairs now stood up in different directions, giving him the look of a hedgehog that'd just been pulled out of its den.

"So, how was it going home for the holidays with *Ellen*? I see ye survived. No parts of ye missing, are there?" His eyes scanned over me, lingering between my legs longer than necessary. I scowled at him, but he just grinned even bigger.

I took it back. I did not miss his meddling self at all.

Focusing back on my task, I scanned the stack for any titles that called the historical fiction shelf their home. It was just my luck that one was located at the bottom of the pile.

"It was fine," I grunted as I moved the top half of the books.

"Fine? That's all I get?"

I shrugged. "Ye ken Ellen. She's not the most open lass."

"I think that may just be *you* she's closed off with. She has no problem talking to me."

I didn't even have to look at him to know his smile was smug. He wasn't wrong, though. He and Ellen had hit it off right away, and she didn't seem to mind spending time with Freya while Doug was around. A spark of jealousy lit up inside me, and I rubbed at my chest in hopes of extinguishing it.

"Well, things may be better between us now. By the end of the day, she seemed...friendly towards me," I admitted.

The sentence felt foreign on my tongue. As long

as I had known Ellen, our interactions had been filled with animosity. The same could be said for our trip, except for at the ruins in Beauly and again that night at the pub.

I'd been beyond pleased when she'd agreed to dance with me. She had looked so dour sitting there at the table watching everyone else have a good time, and I'd doubted either of her brothers would even attempt to get her on the floor. Any other man clearly knew not to approach her, lest he be burned on the spot by her fiery stare.

When we danced, though, it felt just like those few moments outside Mackenzie's tomb; our surroundings fading away until it was only her I saw. Those deep blue irises of hers. There was no tension between us for once, and I found myself relaxing in her presence. We even had a civil conversation without a hint of friction.

"What's that look?"

Doug was out of his chair now, stepping close as he peered at me curiously.

"Fergus, are you...?" He gasped, "Ye actually like her!"

Even though we didn't have any customers at the moment, Mr. Graham shot him a glare from across the room. But Doug didn't pay him a sliver of attention. No, he was completely locked on me. I pushed the cart along, hoping to possibly run over Doug's toes in the process, but no such luck.

"I think the tension between the two of ye is because you're both so bloody attracted to each other. Neither of ye ken how to handle it," he laughed.

I froze. Could he be right? I'd made it clear at supper with the McLeans that I admired Ellen. Her spirit and determination. But oh, how it got under my skin when that fire was directed towards me.

When we'd first met, her tone had been rude and dismissive right away. Even when I'd tried to politely ask her to move elsewhere. There wasn't even an opportunity for me to get to know her before she decided I was an irritating rock in her shoe when, really, she was the boulder in mine. It was *my* routine she had disrupted, *my* table she'd claimed.

No, even if I did think she was beautiful—and beautifully determined as well—Ellen would always hate me. Tolerate me at best. Time had proven such again and again.

"Ellen's made it very clear my presence is an absolute nuisance to her," I argued.

"But ye just said yourself she was friendly to ye. And there was the time ye walked her home in the rain. Sure, she made a couple quips at ye, but ye said ye had a decent conversation over supper."

For once, I struggled to find words. My mouth opened and closed as I started an argument, but then cut it off.

"Well, that doesna mean she finds me attractive or whatever it is you're thinking."

Doug shrugged. "I could always have Freya find out for ye. They're close, and she'd be real subtle about it."

My heart practically sank right down to the soles of my feet. Ellen was clever, and if she figured out what Freya was digging for, I'd never hear the end of it. That's if she ever came near me again. I didn't even know how I felt about her, so I didn't need her thinking there was something between us when there definitely wasn't.

I held up a hand to stop him. "Dougie, please."

I didn't have to say anything more. Just by my tone, he knew I was serious.

"Alright. I'll drop it."

He returned to the chair and allowed me to shelve more books in silence, occupying himself with a random biography he'd plucked from the shelf next to him. I gratefully retreated into the monotony of the task: identify genre, check titles, place book alphabetically by author.

We didn't speak until half of the cart had been restored to their proper places. A few customers had wandered in, but they seemed to be doing fine on their own, so I sat in the chair next to Doug.

"Why didn't ye just wait for me to come home? Were ye that excited to see me?" I teased.

His lips tugged up into a smile, but I could tell he was nervous. My eyebrows knitted together; Doug was rarely unsure of anything.

"I uh-" He rubbed the back of his neck. "I asked my mam for her engagement ring. To give to Freya."

If I hadn't been sitting down, I think I would've collapsed. My eyes were already bugging out of my head. Sure, I knew he wanted to marry her, but actually having a ring was a big step. It was all I could do to keep my voice down so as not to draw attention from the customers.

"When are ye going to propose?" I pressed.

"I dinna quite ken that part yet."

Now I was the one beaming as I clapped a hand on his shoulder. "I'm so happy for ye, Doug. Ye couldna find a greater woman. Especially not one willing to put up with your nonsense."

I winked at him, and he playfully swatted at my hand, causing me to laugh.

"I mean it, though. Freya's wonderful and the two of ye together are"—I glanced around, trying to find the words, before finally gesturing towards the shelves behind him—"something straight out of a novel."

And they had been. Growing up with Doug, I'd seen him around the lasses and in a few short-term relationships. Everything was different with Freya, though. She had the man dressing up and going to plays for goodness' sake.

"Thank ye, Fergus," he smiled shyly. "Ye'll be my best man, of course. I couldna imagine anyone else standing beside me."

My chest filled with warmth. "I'd be honored."

The bell chimed at the counter where a gentleman waited with a couple of books. I stood to help him, glancing over my shoulder at Doug as I went.

"I'll be right back, and then I want to hear more about your holiday break."

He just chuckled and nodded before sinking back

further into the seat. I slipped behind the counter and sent the man a kind smile.

"Afternoon, sir. Did ye find everything ye were looking for?"

"Aye and then some," he chuckled.

"Isn't that how it always goes?"

I recognized one of the books, and we chatted back and forth about it as I rang him up. Just as I handed him his bag, Mr. Graham popped his head out of the office.

"Why don't ye go on and take your break, lad. Catch up with your friend."

He eyed Doug, who was absently tapping his hands against his thighs as he people-watched out the window. I knew what Mr. Graham was really saying. *Take your friend somewhere else.*

"Thank ye, sir. Would ye like anything from the coffee shop? A pastry or tea?" I checked.

He pursed his lips beneath his bushy beard. "Whatever Clara's made fresh."

"Aye, sir."

I made sure everything was set at the register and then made my way back to Doug.

"Come on." I tipped my head towards the door. "Mr. Graham told me to get ye out of here."

His jaw dropped. "He did not!"

"Not in so many words, but I ken the old man well and that's what he was suggesting. Let's go grab a bite and get some coffee so I can survive the rest of this shift."

Doug was still pouting as he followed me out of the shop, sending a pathetic look over his shoulder like a pup being kicked out in the cold.

Only a few other patrons occupied the cafe, so we were able to get our coffee and scones quicker than usual. Doug claimed a table near the back while I grabbed napkins for us.

"How was Hogmanay with Freya in Stirling?" I asked, sliding in across from him.

Doug had been smart and stayed in our hometown for the popular holiday and missed out on the chaotic celebrations here in Edinburgh.

"Very relaxing. Freya just kept saying how much she loves Stirling. She likes the slower pace compared to Edinburgh." He took a sip of his coffee. "I think I'd like that, too. Somewhere out of the city where the bairns would have room to roam."

Out of the city?

It suddenly hit me that once Doug and Freya tied the knot, he would no longer live with me. I'd gotten used to always having him within arm's reach. Even as boys growing up, he lived just down the block. Now here he was discussing moving out of Edinburgh when I planned on spending several more years here, if not staying forever. Edinburgh was a haven for lovers of literature and aspiring authors; the history rich and the inspiration endless.

"Wh-where are ye thinking of moving exactly?" I cleared my throat and then reached for my coffee when it didn't get rid of the hoarseness.

Doug merely shrugged, seemingly clueless to how I felt. "We've mentioned Roslin or possibly even Culross. I wouldna mind living near the water."

Roslin was a mere half hour away, if that. While Culross wasn't much more, I'd prefer my friend to be just on the outskirts of the city. But what say did I have in it? Doug was a grown man and a soon-to-be married one at that. Freya was the one he made his decisions with. Not me.

I mentally scolded myself for being so petty and childish. Freya was also my friend and cared just as dearly for me as I did for her. While change was uncomfortable and sometimes scary, it was a necessary part of life.

When I thought about it, the idea of taking a break from the busy city to visit Doug and Freya in a small village did sound quite lovely. To chase their children around the garden and tell them stories about their father and all the shenanigans we'd gotten up to at their age.

"Well, I suppose it's a good thing I plan on staying in Edinburgh, then. Cannae let ye get too far and leave Freya with the responsibility of looking after ye on her own." I sent a playful wink his way.

Doug scoffed and rolled his eyes before smirking at me. "Admit it. Ye cannae imagine life without me."

I smiled back at him, but it was admittedly shaky.

"No. I can't."

Chapter 11

Ellen

I'd yet to find a course within the biomedical sciences curriculum I did not enjoy. However, Dr. MacTavish was the only professor I enjoyed. The man looked as though he was near retirement, what little hair he had on his head a snowy white just like his beard, but the man was still spritely. I could only hope to be as healthy as he when I reached that age. He was clearly passionate about what he taught and actually taught for understanding, unlike other professors who seemed to teach for the sole purpose of proving how intelligent they were.

When I saw he would be teaching my Clinical Immunology and Haematology course, I was even more excited for the class, a pep in my step despite the early hour. He was standing behind the podium when I entered the lecture hall and looked up from his notes, smiling warmly at me.

"Miss McLean," he greeted. "Pleasure to have you in class again."

I bowed my head in acknowledgement with a polite smile of my own. "I'm looking forward to your lessons, Doctor."

Several other students began to file in behind me, so I moved to find a seat in the front row. As I retrieved my notebook and a pen from my satchel, someone claimed the chair on my left. The lecture hall was only half full, with plenty of seats to choose from, and this lad had chosen the one right next to me. It was a first to be sure. The men in my classes tended to give me a wide berth if they could.

"Hi, I'm William," he smiled, holding out his hand.

I hesitated, but then gave it a confident shake. "Ellen."

"It's nice to meet ye, Ellen." He pushed his glasses further up his nose. "You're about as conspicuous as a peacock, aren't ye?"

"Excuse me?" I raised a brow.

"Sorry." He glanced around the room. "It's just

quite noticeable you're the only lass in here. Is your lad having ye sit in and take notes for him? I wouldn't blame him. Lectures put me to sleep."

"Oh, no," I shook my head. "I'm the one enrolled in this course."

While I'd had plenty of peers surprised to see me in their classes, I'd never had someone assume I was here on behalf of someone else. Did people really do that?

"My apologies," he replied quickly. "So...is that a no on the boyfriend, too?"

I opened and closed my mouth, unsure how to respond, and my cheeks grew warm.

"Yes. I mean, no. I mean..." I closed my eyes to compose myself and then let out a breath before looking at him straight on. "No. I do not have a boyfriend."

"Interesting," he mused, his smile crooked.

He gave me a once-over and I didn't know how to feel under his scrutiny. Before he could say anything else, Dr. MacTavish called for everyone's attention, and I was glad for the redirection of William's gaze.

"Hello, everyone. For those who I don't recognize, I'm Dr. MacTavish. I've been teaching at the university for roughly thirty years now." He raised his hands placatingly. "I know, my good looks are deceiving."

Everyone chuckled.

"Most professors like to spend this first week talking about what you'll be learning. But if it's alright by you, I'd like to get right into things."

He turned and began to write on the chalkboard as he spoke, his voice loud and clear despite his back being towards us. I did my best to make my notes as legible as possible while still keeping up. I'd been doing a considerably good job, in my opinion, when the ink from my pen began to fade. Not wanting to miss anything, I snatched my bag up and began to dig around, hoping to scrounge up another pen.

"Shite," I muttered when I came up empty-handed. Nothing but wrinkled papers and stray crumbs.

"Here."

I looked up to find William proffering a shiny gold pen. I opened my mouth to protest until I saw he had two other pens at the ready. It reminded me of Fergus, sitting in the library with two or three writing utensils neatly lined up next to his notebook.

"Thank ye." I gave William a small smile as I took

the pen from him.

He winked, "Anytime."

My stomach did some weird sort of twist; not terrible, but not pleasant either. While I didn't feel uncomfortable around William, per say, I wasn't sure how to respond to his behavior. Male attention was something I hadn't received since sixth year. It had felt just as peculiar then as it did now.

The gold pen had to be the smoothest writing utensil I had ever used, the ball point gliding effortlessly across the page, and the ink never fading on me once. Dr. MacTavish spoke for the full hour, using up every minute available to him. It wasn't until a student stood and left the room that he even glanced at the clock.

"Oh, I suppose that's time," he smiled sheepishly. "Please read chapter one in your textbooks before next week."

The lecture hall filled with the sounds of shuffling papers and chairs scraping as everyone gathered their things and left. I dropped my notebook into my satchel before regretfully returning the gold pen to William.

"Here ye are. I would've been in trouble without it, so thank ye."

He shook his head. "Keep it."

While part of me wanted to dash away with the pen clutched to my chest lest he change his mind, my parents had taught me manners.

"Are ye sure?" I checked.

"Absolutely. I've got plenty." He patted his bag as if to prove it and then stood, still smiling down at me. "See ye next Monday, Ellen."

I watched his retreating figure, the phrase 'never look a gift horse in the mouth' playing on a loop in my head.

Chapter 12

Fergus

I was practically chomping at the bit to get back into my routine. The moment I stepped into the library, my entire body relaxed. No matter what the rest of this school year held, I was ready to complete it with flying colors like I always did.

Rounding the corner, I was surprised to find my table completely empty. I'd half expected Ellen to be there. Instead, I was actually able to see how the last of the sun's rays turned the wood an almost honey brown, the table completely devoid of stray papers and medical textbooks.

I probably looked odd standing there staring at the table, so I pulled back a chair and got settled in.

It took me no time at all to get my things laid out as I liked. I'd already picked up any books I needed from the front desk, having put them on hold the moment I'd gotten my textbook list. The class I was most excited for was my Scotland and the Supernatural course. My father had always told us folktales and superstitions when we were kids. Scotland was chock-full of them.

Being in Edinburgh, our first topic was Mary King's Close. I had yet to visit the tourist site, but I'd at least heard of it. Like much of Edinburgh, it had its dark history and resulting ghost stories. Not surprising when a whole close is sealed off to trap residents inside during a plague outbreak.

Footsteps approached from behind, and I set my pen down. Normally, I wouldn't pay any mind to other library patrons, but there was a small part of me that hoped it was Ellen. It had been weeks since our night at the pub in her hometown. I hadn't seen her the next morning as she'd still been sleeping when I slipped out of the house, a couple of bannocks from Mrs. McLean in my bag to enjoy on the train.

Doug's 'revelation' had been on my mind, though, and of course, my interactions with Ellen while in Beauly. I was extremely curious to see how she would act around me. Would it be the Ellen who glared and always had a comeback at hand? Or would it be the soft-spoken Ellen, unsure and embarrassed by her dancing abilities?

Alas, it was just some bloke, coming to retrieve a book from the biology section behind me. Returning to my notes, I admonished myself for getting so excited. I wasn't some love-struck teen.

That resolve went out the window when a distinctly female voice gave the man advice on where to find the volume he was looking for. Ellen. I didn't realize I'd been holding my breath until she was standing next to my table. I hesitantly met her eyes and was pleasantly surprised to find a hint of a smile on her lips.

"Fergus," she greeted. "No surprise to find ye here."

My cheeks warmed, and I averted my gaze, busying myself by shifting my books and papers to make room. "There's not much sunlight left, but you're more than welcome to join me if ye'd like."

She hesitated for several—in my opinion—long moments. Had I assumed too much?

"If ye don't mind."

I gestured to the seat across from me. "Not at

all."

She set her bag down on the table to remove what she needed. I'd noticed last semester she would start off fairly organized—for Ellen's standards—but her space would grow progressively more chaotic as she went. Just the thought of it made me itch, especially thinking about how close in proximity I would be to the contagion of her disorder.

As I predicted, her books and papers slowly spread further and further. Like a puddle, seeping outward until something stood in its way and prevented it. Eventually, it encroached on my space.

I tolerated it until she pushed a textbook out of her way with more force than necessary. The tome collided with my own stack of texts and sent the topmost book toppling off the pile and onto my left hand.

"Mmm!" I pressed my lips together to keep a curse from slipping out as I shook my hand, willing away the sharp pain.

"Oh!" Ellen gasped across from me, standing up to peek over her makeshift barricade. "Are ye alright? I'm so sorry, Fergus."

"It's alright. Already feeling better," I lied.

"See, this is why I sit on my own. I always create

a...mess."

I couldn't stop the chuckle that bubbled out of me as I eyed her things. "You're the one who said it, not me."

She did her best to muffle her giggle. If we weren't careful, the librarian would be popping around the corner to threaten us. At least this time it wouldn't be because Ellen and I were arguing.

"I really am sorry, though," Ellen insisted.

She'd sat back down, but her fingers were twiddling in front of her on the table. I stood up enough to reach across the piles of papers and books to place my hand on hers. The fiddling stopped, and I gave her fingers a gentle squeeze, meeting her gaze straight on once she looked up at me.

"And I really am fine," I assured her. "Little harm, little foul."

This time, she practically snorted, even while rolling her eyes. I just smiled.

Arching over the table wasn't the most comfortable, even with my decent height, so I let go and sat back down. I couldn't help but look over the clutter in front of her, doing my best to avoid the graphic illustrations.

"Are there any of these ye dinna need anymore?

I could put them away for ye," I offered.

She scanned her space as well, carefully nudging things this time, before finally closing a couple of the books and stacking them to the side.

"These didna have what I was looking for," she decided.

I simply nodded and stood, coming to her side of the table so I could take them from her.

"Thank ye, Fergus. Ye dinna have to do that. Especially after I smashed your finger." She winced a little, glancing towards the offended digit.

"It's no problem," I shrugged. "I wouldna work at a bookshop if I didna somewhat enjoy shelving books."

I sent her a wink over my shoulder as I headed off to the appropriate shelves. Clearly, this was mostly for my own sake and sanity, but I appreciated that she had allowed me to do something for her with little resistance. That was quite the achievement when it came to Ellen.

It took me no time at all to find the discarded books' rightful places. However, I took a moment's respite to enjoy the orderliness of the looming shelves and their contents. Even if I didn't truly understand the subject they contained, the system of organization was all the same throughout the library.

When I returned to Ellen, it seemed she had done some organization of her own. Her papers were no longer sprawled across the mahogany, instead placed in three piles.

"I dinna think ye'll be offering to share a table with me anymore," she confessed shyly.

"Och," I waved my hand dismissively as I sat down in my seat. "Maybe over time I'll rub off on ye and ye'll finally have a system to your madness."

She scoffed, and I was admittedly pleased to hear it. "I do have a system. I ken well where everything is at."

I just eyed her skeptically. "Aye. If ye say so."

Ellen huffed in response, and I half expected her to cross her arms over her chest like a disgruntled toddler.

I'd barely read more than two words when Ellen cleared her throat, the chair creaking under her as she shifted.

"I meant to ask ye about your manuscript ye interviewed my mam for. Did her stories help ye any?"

The mention of my book had me perking up

instantly. "Aye, it did. I believe her insight added a great deal to the story. Please send along my gratitude the next time ye speak to her."

"I will," she promised. "Is there any chance—" She hesitated and shook her head. It seemed I was, in fact, getting the soft-spoken Ellen today. "Ye can say no, but...I'd love to read what ye have so far."

My chest swelled with pride. As any author could agree, it was a great feeling to have someone eager to read your writing.

"Of course. It's at home, but I could bring it with me this week if you're sure of a day ye'll be here."

She shook her head quickly. "Oh, dinna do that. There's no need to drag it all the way here."

Ellen already knew where I lived, having attended the house party Doug had hosted. However, the idea of her being there to see me— correction: my manuscript—was quite hallucinatory. I couldn't suggest such a thing. I didn't think I'd survive.

"I work at the bookshop on Thursday. It wouldna be any trouble at all to bring it with me if ye'd like to meet me there."

"Aye. That sounds like a good plan to me," Ellen smiled.

It wasn't an expression I'd seen on her often and it made my heart do this odd thing in my chest. Something it hadn't done in years.

As if there'd been some silent cue exchanged, we both went back to our own books. For the next hour, our space was only filled with the sounds of pages turned and notes scribbled into journals.

When my usual three hours were up, I actually hesitated, not wanting to leave. It had been a pleasant afternoon with Ellen, and I was content to stay in this little bubble of quiet comradery. But I had my routine, and if I wasn't home within the half hour, Doug would be sending a search party out for me. I'd also probably get an earful for not being there to assist with supper. He'd specifically requested chicken stovies tonight, feeling nostalgic for home-cooked meals after the holiday break. However, Doug had never been able to prepare chicken properly without making it dry or chewy, so that part was left to me.

Just the idea of supper had my stomach threatening to rumble, so I quickly stacked my books and tucked my things into my leather satchel.

"Well." I stood, but hesitated, eyes everywhere except on Ellen. But then I caught sight of a detailed drawing of the human brain and, in fear of losing my appetite, met her loch blue eyes. "I best be heading home for supper."

"Oh." Now it was her turn to check her watch. "Of course."

I lingered, getting the sense there was more she wanted to say, but maybe that was just because I'd never known Ellen to say so little.

"Thank ye for sharing the table with me, and I'm sorry again about your hand."

"Och, it's fine now," I quickly dismissed her apology.

Her lips pursed together in a thin line, but she nodded her head before attempting another smile. "Aye, well. I suppose I'll see ye Thursday then. At Graham's Bookshop."

"Aye, I'll be sure to remember the manuscript."

An awkward tension rippled between us, having replaced the comfortable feeling of the last hour. There was nothing else to say, so I merely tipped my head to her before turning and exiting the library. Despite the stinted goodbye, I felt very pleased with the evening overall. Maybe we were over our quarreling.

Chapter 13

Ellen

A kaleidoscope of butterflies had decided to take residence in my stomach as I made my way to Graham's Bookshop. While Fergus and I had seemingly come to a truce, being around him still unnerved me. Which was ridiculous given the man had stayed in my childhood home and I'd danced wrapped up in his arms.

I quickly shook my head to rid it of the memory. One so visceral, it was as if I could feel his arms around me at that very moment. That was not a feeling I needed to dwell on. No, reading his manuscript in his workplace would not be as personal as that. It's not as though he would stand over my shoulder and watch me as I read. He had a job to do after all. I was only here because it was more convenient for him, and I was curious to see how much of my mother he'd put in his story.

I saw the hanging sign for the bookshop up ahead, and my steps slowed. Like a feral cat backed into a corner by a dog, my eyes scanned the street for an escape. Or at least a means of delay. I spotted the cafe across the road and decided a cup of tea was exactly what I needed to calm my nerves.

I jogged across the mostly empty street, hoping Fergus wouldn't see me through the bookshop windows slipping into the cafe. The scent of steeping tea leaves and ground coffee beans instantly enveloped me, and my whole body seemed to melt as if I was the one with steaming water being poured over me.

A handful of patrons were scattered throughout the shop, either chatting or reading in a secluded corner. I subconsciously wondered if the gentleman reading had just purchased his book at Graham's. Had Fergus recommended it?

I forced myself to focus on the menu instead of thinking about his kind smile. I needed to get a grip on myself before I faced him.

"Hullo. How can I help ye?" a young lass asked from behind the counter, her blonde hair pulled back to show off her moss green eyes.

"Hi. Can I have a lavender tea, please?"

I didn't have an idea of what tea Fergus preferred, so I found myself eyeing the baked goods in the display counter instead. Not like I knew his preference of scone flavor either.

"I'd recommend the cranberry-orange scones," the girl suggested, noticing the direction of my gaze. "They've been very popular this winter."

That sounded good enough. "Aye, I'll take two, then. Thank ye."

I passed her a handful of notes before she'd even shared the total, having already tallied it up in my mind from what was on the menu.

"Keep the change as a tip," I urged when she started to count it out.

Those green eyes met mine and seemed to brighten with her smile. "Oh. Thank ye verra much, ma'am."

I smiled politely and then stepped to the side to wait for my things, unable to keep myself from glancing across the street. It looked like any other bookshop, nothing extraordinary about it. Except for the charming man working inside.

I really needed to get my snowballing feelings under control before they turned into an avalanche. Fergus was only being nice to me after I'd done the favor of setting up his interview with my mother. Add on our mutual friends, and it was better for us to not be constantly at each other's throats.

"Here ye are, dearie."

The blonde passed me my warm cup and a brown paper bag containing the scones. I thanked her once more. There was no more putting it off, then. I needed to buckle down and get my arse over there.

I waited for a cab to pass and then hurried across, taking a moment to compose myself before I pushed the door open with my elbow. A bell chimed above my head, but the older gentleman at the register didn't even flinch. Had he not heard, or was he simply unbothered?

I wasn't the only visitor after all. A toddler held onto his mother's fingers as she scanned a shelf, lips pursing when she pulled one down to glance through. Another gentleman sat in an armchair by the window with a large tome opened flat in his lap, spectacles in danger of slipping off his long nose. Then I saw Fergus.

He entered through some doorway in the back with an armful of books, but then he saw me and stopped, a smile spreading across his face. I stayed rooted in my spot even as he approached me.

"Hi."

"I brought you a scone," I blurted. His eyes darted to the paper bag in my grasp. "I didna ken what ye'd like, but the lass behind the counter recommended these."

His smile grew. "Ah, so ye met Moira, then."

They're on a first-name basis.

The knowledge of that made the butterflies in my stomach twitch irritably. I tried to reason that she had looked quite young; surely younger than Fergus and me.

"Let me just put these away, and I'll get the manuscript." He gestured towards a set of leather chairs in a back corner. "Have a seat and I'll meet ye there."

I glanced towards the older man again. "He willna mind us eating near the books?"

Fergus followed my gaze and then chuckled, shaking his head. "Och, no. I cannae tell ye the number of times I've caught Mr. Graham munching on one of Clara's scones while he works. Swear that's why the number five key on the register is so finicky."

He walked to the shelf the young mother had just been at. Left alone, I had no choice but to move to the chairs in the back, lest I stand there and block the entryway like a dafty.

The whisky brown leather was cool, even through the wool of my skirt. I set the bag of scones on the table and finally took a sip of my tea. My nerves had returned, and I needed the magical, calming effects of the lavender. Now.

I found myself tracking Fergus' confident movements throughout the store. He clearly knew exactly where each book went, gently nudging it between its companions. While the owner barely gave more than a few grumbled responses to the woman and her son as they checked out, Fergus intercepted the mother before they left.

"Is it alright if I give him a sweet?" He tipped his head towards the child.

"Oh, he'd love that," she smiled brightly. "Thank ye."

Fergus kneeled down to the boy's level, proffering him a sweet from his pocket. The toddler's eyes rounded, completely locked on the shiny wrapper as he reached out a chubby little hand to take it.

"Oh, well, look at that, Billy," his mother cooed. "Can ye thank the nice lad?"

He had already managed to discard the wrapper and shove the treat into his mouth, a bit of drool leaking out of the corner of his lips as his wide eyes met Fergus'. "Ank you."

Fergus chuckled as he ruffled the lad's hair. "You're very welcome, Billy. Come back soon, aye?"

He stood up straight to wave them off. I quickly averted my gaze when he walked past me to the backroom, not wanting him to know I'd been watching. It took only a few moments for him to return with his manuscript in one hand and a coffee cup in the other.

I frowned at the mug. "I would've gotten ye tea, but I didna ken what ye liked."

"Och, dinna fash. Ye brought me a scone and ye didna have to do that." He settled into the other chair and then peeked into the paper bag. "And ye got my favorite!"

I raised a brow questionably. "Cranberry-orange is your favorite?"

"What's wrong with cranberry-orange?" he

challenged.

"Nothing," I shrugged. "Just an interesting choice for your favorite."

He snagged one of the scones and wiggled back into his seat. "It's my favorite winter flavor, at least. The baker, Clara, is always coming up with new flavors each season. I dinna think I could pick an overall favorite."

It had taken us no time at all to fall into old habits, and I found the familiarity of our banter a relief.

Fergus' scone was gone in the blink of an eye. I'd barely taken a bite of my own—the flavor admittedly delicious—before he was dusting the crumbs off his lap.

"Alright then." He picked up the manuscript from the table between us and began to page through it. "I truly cannae thank your mam enough. The scenes where the main character suffers a major injury are so much more vivid now—and accurate, I'm sure."

I smiled softly, "Well, I ken she enjoyed sharing her stories with ye, even if they're heavy."

He returned my small smile and nodded. Then he held out the pages, and I quickly set down my tea to free my hands. How he had found brads big enough to contain the pile was beyond me. The paper was crisp and fresh, clearly having been recently printed. I retrieved a pen from my purse.

"Do ye mind?" I asked, hesitating a moment.

Fergus waved his hand, "Not at all. The more feedback I can get, the better."

The chiming of the bell and sudden whoosh of cool, damp air signaled the arrival of a customer, and Fergus let out a sigh. "Suppose, I'd better get back to work and leave ye to it."

He pushed himself up from the chair, taking his mug with him as he disappeared into the backroom once more. I sank back into the armchair, relieved to be alone. More specifically, away from him. I already hadn't been thinking right since holiday break, and being in his presence made it distinctly worse.

Focus, Ellen, I scolded myself.

The reason I was here was to read his manuscript, to see how he'd intertwined the stories of my mother's experiences in the war with whatever story he was trying to share. Usually, I found fictional pieces to be boring. They often started slow and took far too long to pick up for my attention span. I'd given up on them long ago and stuck to my medical texts, which were far more interesting in my opinion.

However, I found myself hooked by Fergus' story within the first paragraph. He didn't bother with pages of tiresome background information about the characters and their current situation. Instead, he threw the reader right into the deep end.

Fergus had a way of painting a mental image as vivid as if I were at the picture show watching it play out on a giant screen. Maybe it was because I'd heard my mother talk about the war and what she'd seen ever since I was a bairn, but it was more likely Fergus was just that talented. I could feel what the characters were feeling; their emotions palpable through the ink. It made it so I hung on every word and read as fast as possible so I could figure out what happened next.

I was only partially aware of customers coming and going, the door chime and tapping of the register keys fading into the background as I got lost in the world Fergus had created. The sun had been down for a while, the bookshop bathed in warm light from the lamps scattered about, when he rejoined me, sitting down in the chair with a tired sigh. I was barely halfway through the script, but I finished the current chapter before finally pulling myself from the world I'd spent the last couple of hours in.

"What do ye think so far?"

"Fergus," I gushed, unable to find the words at the moment. My tone of voice must have made it clear just how impressed I was, because a flush crept above his collar, and the shy smile he graced me with was the most endearing thing I'd ever seen. "I'm going to be blatantly honest in telling you I am not a fiction reader, but...this? I couldn't stop."

He just turned even redder, ducking into the seat next to me, eyes trained on the table between us.

"Do ye mean it, Ellen?" he asked finally, nails picking at the arm of the chair as he peeked up at me. "Ye aren't just gassing me up to get a rise out of me, are ye?"

My smile slipped. It bothered me that he thought I would lie to him.

"Fergus. I wouldna do that to ye. I ken how hard you've worked on this."

The hours he spent bent over his manuscript in the library, completely unaware of my gaze on him or the coming and going of other students. How excited he'd been when he found out my mother had served in the war. Just the way he spoke of his story, with reverence and adoration, made it painfully apparent how much this piece meant to him.

I placed my hand over his without thinking. "I mean it, Fergus," I spoke softly, but unwaveringly. I didn't want him to have even a sliver of doubt in my sincerity. "This is an incredible story."

His face was completely bare to me, every thought and emotion as easy to read as the words on the pages of the books surrounding us. The crease between his brows smoothed out, and his eyes softened. Fergus turned his hand in mine, and I held my breath when he interlaced our fingers. His grip was barely there, allowing me to remove my hand if I wanted to, but the thing was...I didn't. Not even in the slightest.

"Thank ye, Ellen."

"Fergus!"

We both jumped, breaking apart at the sudden interruption. My hands settled the manuscript in my lap to keep it from falling onto the floor. Prior to now, I hadn't thought the old man capable of such volume or clarity.

"It's about time to lock up. Bid your lassie goodbye, and then I need ye to close down the register," he instructed.

"Yes, Mr. Graham," Fergus nodded.

I quickly tucked my pen, which had gone completely ignored the entire evening, into my purse and carefully closed the manuscript before passing it to Fergus. We both stood at the same time, which led to an awkward tango of determining who would go first. Fergus finally gestured for me with a sweep of his hand and then followed me to the door.

I paused in the entryway like I had upon my arrival earlier this evening, once again flustered and unsure of what to say. "Thank ye again for letting me read it. I'd love to finish it sometime."

"Of course. Ye ken where to find me most evenings."

"Bookshop or the library," I confirmed. "Easy enough."

He laughed under his breath.

"Mam will be very excited to get her hands on a copy once it's published."

"Ye mean *if* it gets published." He smiled self-deprecatingly, which just made me shake my head more firmly.

"No. When."

His expression softened and so did his eyes. Oh, what a beautiful sapphire they were. Almost like the night sky at sunset, when the stars were beginning to make their debut, whether the sun was ready to share the stage or not.

Without breaking our gaze, he reached around me to open the door. I shivered at the cool air, tempted to take a step closer to him, but I forced myself to back out onto the pavement.

"Goodnight, Ellen," he spoke softly, his voice almost drowned out by a passing car.

"Goodnight, Fergus."

Chapter 14

Fergus

February

I had never been so proud of myself for having the foresight to wear a dark shirt. Sweat droplets trickled down the nape of my neck and under my collar. The Top Storey dance hall was filled to the brim with dolled-up lassies and lads following them around like puppy dogs. It seemed as if everyone from the university had shown up for the hall's last hoorah before it closed for good.

I had partnered with Freya for several of the more upbeat songs, Doug unfortunately being burdened with the disease of two-left-footitis;

incurable despite my best efforts over the years. He wasn't completely hopeless, though, at least capable of a simple step-touch for the slow songs. When he wasn't stiffly waltzing Freya around the floor, he held down a table for us just on the outskirts of the crowd.

Freya and I practically held each other up as we pushed through the mass of bodies to Doug. I didn't think I'd ever been so happy to see a glass of water in my life, eagerly downing it all before my arse had even hit the seat.

"Dougie, please go back with me for the next dance. Give poor Fergus a break," Freya urged, gently tugging on his sleeve.

"But he's doing such a nice job," Doug argued. "I dinna want to embarrass ye."

Freya scoffed and rolled her eyes. "There are so many people out there, nobody can tell the difference."

She wasn't wrong. The floor was growing more packed as the night went on. It was surprising anyone was able to actually dance at all. We'd bumped into our fair share of couples, even with our decent footwork.

Either way, I knew Doug would give in to her. He

was completely wrapped around Freya's finger and would do anything she asked of him.

"Alright, alright. I'll dance with ye, but drink more of your water. Last thing I need is ye passing out on me."

That earned him a kiss from Freya, and then she did as he asked, drinking her water in a much more civilized fashion than I had. The three of us sat there, just enjoying the music for a while before Freya suddenly sat up straight, eyebrows pinching together.

"Is that Ellen?"

I practically cracked my neck turning to look, eyes scanning the crowd. The dance hall was the last place I would expect to see Ellen. She'd made it clear in Beauly she wasn't comfortable on a dance floor and had little faith in her abilities. It was a miracle I'd gotten her to join me that night at the pub.

But there she was. Dancing. In the arms of another man.

My stomach bottomed out as I watched them. He was about as tall as me, but much thinner, which led to him being a touch awkward on the dance floor. He collided with a couple behind them, and Ellen just giggled as she pushed his spectacles back up his nose. Never had I heard Ellen McLean giggle before.

Had she ever smiled at me like that? Her eyes sparkling like the sun glistening off the surface of the loch? Surely not.

"Oi. Ye'll pop a blood vessel staring that hard," Doug mumbled under his breath with a firm nudge to my ribs.

"I wasna–"

He and Freya just wore matching expressions of disbelief that had me flushing once more, and not from the heat of the room.

"Do you know who he is?" Freya asked gently, directing the question to both me and Doug. "She's never mentioned anyone to me before."

I just shook my head, clearly rendered speechless by the unfathomable sight in front of me. My friends debated theories next to me, but their words didn't register. In all honesty, it didn't matter who he was. I hated him either way for the simple fact that he was the recipient of Ellen's startling smile.

The band ended with a flourish, and everyone applauded, couples leaving the dance floor in search of refreshments while others quickly took their place for the next song. The man leaned down to whisper in her ear. Sweet nothings?

I watched as Ellen nodded and he gave her elbow a squeeze before disappearing into the crowd. Left alone, her eyes scanned the hall before landing on our table. Her expression brightened as she made her way towards us.

"Hi there!" she exhaled.

Freya stood and pulled Ellen into a hug. "I didn't expect to see you here."

I averted my gaze, suddenly interested in the condensation lingering on my empty glass.

"Oh. Well..." I could hear the shyness in her voice, and I hated that I knew what that sounded like. Hated even more the bloke responsible for it. "Figured I couldna be the only one from uni who didna come."

I watched from the corner of my eye as she took the empty seat next to Freya.

"Who's your date?" Doug asked.

I didn't wait for Ellen to answer and shoved my chair back as I stood. "I'm going out for some air."

If any of them said anything in response, it was drowned out by the trumpeter's solo.

I skirted along the edge of the hall until I reached a door leading to the alleyway at the back of the building. The heavy door closed behind me, muffling the music and chatter inside significantly. I was grateful for the reprieve; my thoughts were loud enough.

A group of lads had gathered just left of the stoop, so I stepped down and turned in the other direction. I was in the midst of racking my brain for any sort of distraction to keep me from thinking about Ellen when I heard her name mentioned by one of the men. I froze.

Surely, they're speaking about another Ellen. It's a common enough name.

Still, I found myself straining to hear the rest of their conversation.

"I can't believe ye got the hackit to come with ye. Any man that so much as glances in her direction gets the glare of Medusa."

"You're either the bravest man I know, William, or the stupidest."

"Och, all it took was a little sweet talking. She's just like any other lass, desperate for a compliment. And I wasna about to turn down the chance at twenty quid."

My fingers curled into fists. Ellen wasn't so simple, and she was not some air-headed lass. The woman was absolutely brilliant. And these here gowks were placing bets on who could get her to come to the dance with them.

"Surely telling her she's bonnie didn't work."

"No, I lied out my arse about how smart she is. Knew that'd gas her up right quick." They all laughed at this. "I tell ye, the lass is downright delusional if she thinks she's going to have a career in the medical field. 'Tis a place for men. Not these frail females."

That sealed it. There wasn't an ounce of doubt in my mind that they were talking about my Ellen. All reasoning went out the window as I stalked over to them.

"If anyone is frail around here, it's a man who talks shite about a woman to make himself feel better."

He was only an inch or so shorter, but I made sure to stretch to my fullest height when he turned around to face me.

"Och, come on," he laughed. "Ye ken I'm right."

I shook my head. "I cannae say I'm of the same mind. And I'd appreciate it if ye kept Ellen's name out of your mouth."

His lips twisted into a vile sneer. "I can say what I want. She's my date, after all, and the wee besom is eating out of the palm of my hand. She's so starved for a man's attention." He turned back to his friends who were only egging him on. "I'm sure she'll be beggin' me to–"

I didn't allow him to finish his sentence. I gripped his shoulder and spun him around, managing to catch the look of confusion on his face just before my right fist connected with his nose, creating a satisfying crunch. Whether it was his glasses, his nose, or my knuckles that made the sound, I couldn't be sure. My blood pulsed in my ears with a roar that blocked everything out, and I probably looked like a crazed animal standing above him as he doubled over, cradling his face in his hands.

"You stay away from Ellen, ye hear me?" I turned on all the others, the smug smiles wiped off their faces now as they huddled together like sheep. "All of ye. Ye only wish ye were as talented as she is."

"Fergus!"

It was Freya who had cried out, and her scream was like a bucket of cold water poured over my head, clearing away the rage. The others scrambled to get their friend off the ground, blood streaming from his nose until he pressed the back of his hand to it, but that only made him wince. Maybe I had broken it. Served him right.

He managed a glare in my direction before the mob of them disappeared down the alleyway. I couldn't be sure they'd leave Ellen alone completely, but at least they knew they had more to fear than her menacing glower.

I hissed when Freya touched my hand and jerked it back, whipping around to face her.

"You're bleeding," she admonished. "What on earth were you thinking?"

"They were speaking ill of Ellen. The piece of shite that brought her tonight was bragging about how he'd won some bet, getting her to come with him, and how he was going to-"

"I could have handled it myself."

Ellen was standing in the doorway, backlit by the lights of the chandeliers, but I could see she had her arms crossed tightly over her chest and jaw set firm.

I let out a sigh. I didn't want to fight with her. The anger and adrenaline that had surged in me so suddenly had left just as abruptly. Of course, she was mad at me for standing up for her again.

"I ken that well. And if ye were here, I would have let ye at him and called out everyone to watch ye beat the bawbag. But ye werena and I didna have the patience to wait for ye to find us. He needed someone to hit him right then."

My gaze broke from hers when Freya pressed a handkerchief to the cut on my knuckles, and I muttered a curse under my breath. His glasses must have gotten me. I hoped I'd broken them as well as his nose, if only to inconvenience him further.

"Let me look at him."

Ellen stepped up beside Freya and took my hand in hers much more carefully. I managed not to flinch as she tilted it this way and that to examine it in what little light there was.

"Nothing seems broken, at least, and ye dinna need stitches." She replaced the handkerchief and made quick work of tying it around my palm to keep it in place. "They'll be bloody sore for a while, though, I'm sure."

I simply made a noise deep in the back of my throat in response, eyes turned down away from her.

"I'm going to find Dougie so we can leave," Freya announced, disappearing back into the hall now that I was in capable hands.

I waited until the door closed behind her to

finally look at Ellen. Her arms were once more crossed, and her lips set in a straight line as she stared off down the alley where the men had disappeared.

"Why did ye even agree to go with him?" I blurted.

It was something I had been trying to wrap my mind around ever since I saw them dancing.

"I only said yes because *you* never asked me," she answered sharply.

"Och, so it's my fault ye came with the eejit then, is it?"

For once, she didn't fight back. She just stared at me with a look I didn't recognize.

I'd seen the stormy seas of her eyes when she was heated, the fire that burned in them. I'd also seen the eerily still waters with a kelpie lurking beneath the surface, just waiting for you to come close enough they could drown you. No, this was a drizzle on the loch, water rippling from the raindrops. She meant it, and I'd upset her.

"I figured you'd reject me," I admitted.

She was quiet for only a moment and then she made a noise of frustration through her nose. "Bloody idiot," she muttered.

Before I could open my mouth to defend myself, she had firmly planted her hands on either side of my face and pulled me down, her lips crashing into mine. I stumbled forward, only keeping myself up by grabbing onto her waist; the sting in my knuckles barely registering as my lips melted against hers and the important facts fell into place.

Ellen was kissing me. Ellen was upset that I hadn't asked her to the dance. Ellen had feelings for me.

My grip on her tightened, and I pulled her closer to my chest. The pleased sound she made against my mouth sent a chill down my spine, but I swore my body was on fire.

"Fergus, El–"

We tore apart to find Doug and Freya standing in the alley doorway wearing similar expressions of astonishment. However, Doug's quickly morphed into a massive grin, too big for his face.

"About damn time! Michty me."

Now Freya was beaming, "I knew it!"

Ellen started to laugh, then, sufficiently breaking the tension that had permeated the alleyway. Her body completely sank into mine as we all joined in. If the last hour had been a thrill ride, I was currently in the freefall, feeling lighter than air with that giddy twist in my stomach that belied a mix of fear and excitement.

I wrapped my arm more securely around Ellen and placed a kiss to the top of her head when she rested it against my shoulder.

Ellen

I slipped my heels off, more than grateful to be rid of the horrendous things, and wiggled my toes in my stockings before tucking my feet back up under my skirt. The cool night was a stark contrast to the overheated dance hall, but I much preferred being here, nestled between the roots of a giant elm tree with Fergus. Oh, what a turn the night had taken.

When I glanced up at him, I found his eyes already on me and his lips curved into a gentle smile. I still wasn't used to the way this man made me feel. Never had anyone made me, Ellen McLean, bashful, but I knew my cheeks were burning and could only hope the dark blanket of night hid the severity of it.

"How many times can I say I'm sorry?"

I pursed my lips in playful thought as I rested my head back against the solid trunk. "I'd say forty more times may have ye covered."

He pinched my side, and I flinched away, but his arms were pulling me back into him within seconds, both of us giggling.

This time, his lips were pressed to my temple as he whispered, "I'm so sorry."

I nuzzled further into him. "I'm sorry, too. I've given ye all the reasons to think I would have said no."

I'd never known Fergus to be afraid of anything save an interruption to his rigid routine. To think I had such power over him and his emotions was baffling. Sure, I knew it was easy for me to rile him up, but I never could have imagined igniting a feeling of passion in him in a different way. Clearly, I had been wrong.

His hand found mine, and I watched as he toyed with my fingers, tapping along each pad as if playing the piano. He was so gentle, and I was quickly learning that was Fergus at his core: a kind and caring man. Funny how we started off with such wrong impressions of each other.

"To think if I'd just given ye back your table that first evening, this all could have gone very differently."

He laughed then, a deep and hearty rumble in his chest. "Aye, but it was fun, no? Ye cannae tell me ye havena enjoyed pestering me."

Now it was my turn to laugh, knowing I couldn't deny it.

"Och, no. It's quite entertaining to watch ye get your knickers in a twist," I smirked up at him.

"So that part isn't going to change. Noted."

"Wouldna be us if it did."

"Aye," he chuckled.

It was a relief to know our relationship wouldn't be completely different now that our feelings were out there. Or I at least assumed my affection was clear; I had kissed the bloke after all. But I supposed we hadn't outright declared anything.

I intertwined our fingers, stilling his movements and directing his attention back to solely me. In just a silent exchange, he seemed to have read my mind.

"I ken we're familiar enough with each other, but I'd like to do this properly, Ellen." His hold on me tightened ever so slightly. "I'd like to take ye on a date tomorrow evening, if that's alright with you."

"It is more than alright with me," I beamed. "I'd love that, Fergus."

His smile matched my own, and he let go of my hand to cup my cheek. I leaned into his warm touch, wondering idly how I had ever found this man so infuriating.

"If I'm doing this properly, does that mean I should wait until tomorrow to kiss ye again?" he asked, his breath a mere whisper across my lips.

"Absolutely not."

I'd initiated the first kiss in the alleyway, but it was Fergus who took the lead this time, tilting my chin up as he leaned down to press his lips to mine. This kiss was more gentle, more exploratory. Our first had been so spur of the moment, I hadn't had the chance to fully enjoy what was happening before we were interrupted. Now it was only us. All of Edinburgh asleep, and the world quiet except for the soft rustling of the leaves above as the serene elm stood sentry over us.

Chapter 15

Ellen

"Would you please sit *still*?" Freya huffed.

"Well, if ye'll stop stabbing me with the wee bobbies, I will!"

She'd offered to style my hair for my date tonight, and I regretted it once she'd started pinning the curls in place. I was one to keep things simple, but that definitely was not Freya's style. At least I was capable of doing my own makeup and didn't have to run the risk of Freya poking my eye out. My scalp would be tender enough.

"Do you know where he's taking you?" she asked, finally stepping away.

"No. I was actually hoping you'd ken his plans."

"Surprisingly, Dougie has kept his mouth shut. I'm assuming Fergus was smart enough not to tell him. Dougie can never keep a secret, bless him."

I had to fight my grin, knowing of a particular secret Dougie was actually doing a remarkably excellent job of keeping to himself. Or at least keeping from Freya.

Freya's hands on my shoulders brought me back, and I smiled at her in the mirror.

"You look stunning, Ellen. Fergus won't know what to do with himself."

My cheeks turned pink, but I did my best to keep my eyes on hers, forcing myself to accept the compliment.

"Thank you, Freya," I murmured, reaching up to place my hand over hers.

The clock on my desk showed I only had ten minutes before I was expected to meet Fergus outside the dormitory. He was probably already downstairs. "I best be getting down there. I dinna need him heckling me for being late. Ye ken Fergus and his need for punctuality."

Freya's eyes widened in understanding as she moved to the vanity. "Think it actually physically pains the man to be late."

I stood to help her gather her things, but she shooed me away.

"I'll clean up here. You go on before he starts to panic, thinking you've stood him up."

Wanting to start out on the right foot, I followed Freya's instructions and grabbed my purse before heading out of my room. Just as I expected, Fergus was already there, casually leaning against the stone railing, eyes fixed on his timepiece.

"Made it with time to spare, didn't I?" I smirked down at him, only smiling wider when he startled, head snapping up and eyes wide.

"Aye, ye did," he chuckled.

His body relaxed, and he confidently held his hand out to assist me down the stairs. Normally, I would refuse such chivalry as I was more than capable of making it on my own, even in heels, but Freya's voice rang in my head that I needed to allow him to be a gentleman. I couldn't say I disliked the feel of his hand in mine, sturdy yet gentle.

As we started towards the edge of campus, he tucked my hand into the crook of his arm, moving slowly as if he might startle me. I gave his bicep a quick squeeze of reassurance and smiled up at him for good measure.

"So are ye going to tell me where we're going?"

"I thought ye might enjoy going to the picture show," he answered. I opened my mouth to respond, but he held up his free hand to halt me. "I didna figure ye were keen on a romance, so I've instead gotten us tickets to see *The Miracle Worker*."

My steps hesitated. "The one about Anne Sullivan's work with Hellen Keller?"

"Aye. I assumed ye'd enjoy it, what with your medical mind, and I'm quite partial to pictures based on true stories myself."

The butterflies—that I was growing quite accustomed to—fluttered in my chest, overly pleased at how much thought he'd put into his choice. How much consideration he'd taken of my interests.

"Sounds absolutely wonderful."

His smile brightened, and I couldn't help but find the expression utterly adorable on his handsome face.

We chatted mindlessly as we walked, in no great rush. Fergus asked about my family, and I regaled him with the latest updates from my brothers, Fin having finally introduced his Welsh lass to our parents.

"How long do ye think until he proposes to her

then?" Fergus lifted a dark brow.

"Oh, months at most. It's terribly disgusting how smitten they are. Almost as bad as Dougie and Freya," I laughed. "Has Dougie decided when he'll pop the question?"

Fergus playfully rolled his eyes as he let out a dramatic sigh. "He may have kent right away he wanted to marry her, but he is being so indecisive about how to do it. He'll probably end up blurting it out over tea instead of one of the grandiose plans he's prattled on about."

"I believe Freya would be just as happy with that as anything. All that matters to her is that he asks."

His eyes widened slightly. "Agreed. And I've told Doug as much."

"He'll figure it out," I assured him.

We turned the corner, and the theater marquee lit up half the street. Given that Fergus had already purchased our tickets, we were able to skip the line and go directly inside.

"Popcorn is on me and any sweets ye'd like," he offered.

"But ye've already purchased the tickets. Let me cover our treats," I insisted.

Fergus opened his mouth to argue, but then

thought better of it. I beamed at him as we joined the queue, more than pleased he was allowing me to pay for him. Other men would never allow a woman to cover the cost of something on a date, but Fergus was a smart man.

"You're learning," I teased.

He playfully scoffed next to me. "Aye. I ken which battles are worthless to fight with ye. Best to let ye have your way. This time."

His emphasis on 'this time' didn't go unnoticed, but I'd leave that for a later date. He'd come around soon enough.

Treats secured, Fergus led the way into the theater, finding us seats as close to the middle of the row as possible.

"What sweets did ye choose?" he asked, eyeing the bag in my hands.

"Sherbet lemons. Tart sweeties are my favorite."

I held them out to him in offering and let a few pieces tumble into the palm of his hand. He unwrapped one before popping it into his mouth. Within seconds, his lips pursed, and one of his eyes squinted shut.

"Mm-mm," he shook his head, eyeing me as he crunched the hard-shelled sweet to consume it faster.

I tried my best not to laugh at him. "Ye could've just said no thanks. Ye didna have to take it if ye kent ye didna like it."

"Thought I might handle it better now that I've grown."

This time, it was I who took the liberty of hooking my hand into Fergus' elbow as we exited the theater.

"I still cannae wrap my mind around the patience of that woman. To not only stay relatively calm given the behaviors of Helen, but then to teach her language and how to sign. It's astounding!"

"She's lucky it wasna Ellen McLean who came to teach her."

My jaw dropped and I playfully whacked my free hand against his arm as he laughed wickedly, head tossed back.

"Oi! What are ye saying?"

"Oh, be honest. Ye would've walked out of there the second she snagged a bannock off your plate," he eyed me with a smirk.

I kept my mouth shut, knowing he was more than correct. I wouldn't have lasted a minute with the girl.

"Ye may be stubborn, but ye willna put up with disrespect," he reasoned. "And I cannae say I wouldna do the same."

Despite our rocky start, we'd clearly learned a good deal about each other. Maybe it was better that way, to see the worst of somebody first so you knew what you were getting into. We'd at least learned what *not* to do if we wanted to avoid setting the other off. But I'd like to think there were positive attributes along the way as well, such as Fergus' work ethic and his confidence in speaking up for what he believed. The man wore his heart on his sleeve and it was a trait I was envious of. I could stand to learn from him.

Fergus nudged me gently. "Ye went somewhere else."

"Oh." I blushed, ducking my head so a loose curl fell between us. "Just thinking of how much we've learned about each other. Given our...abysmal beginnings."

He seemed to ponder the sentiment for a

moment, our footsteps and the rattling of passing cars the only sounds, before he responded. "Aye, but we're making up for it, no?"

I looked up to meet his gentle gaze and smiled shyly. "Aye. I'd like to think so."

A roll of thunder was the only warning before the skies opened and released a downpour.

"Shite!" Fergus cursed.

He hurried to remove his suit coat to hold above us in a vain attempt to keep dry. All I could do was laugh as we hurried along the cobblestones until we found an alcove in the entryway of a shop to take refuge in. Fergus glared out at the rain, which just made me laugh more.

"Oi, it's no funny," he grumbled, but I could tell he wasn't actually mad at me. "We were having a nice walk."

"It's very funny," I argued.

It was only then that I realized how close we were, still huddled under his coat despite the protection of the awning above us. The streetlights sent half of his face into shadow, but I found myself lost in his eyes nevertheless. It was like that moment in the Beauly Priory all over again. Some indescribable connection that erased our surroundings and left only each other in high definition.

I couldn't say who initiated the kiss or if we both leaned in at the same time, him down and me up as I pushed onto my toes, hands braced against his solid chest. For such a bookish man, he was quite fit, and I couldn't keep myself from noting and appreciating it.

The kiss started off gentle, but then I felt his tongue swipe across my bottom lip and found myself parting my lips to greet it with my own. He finally abandoned his coat, lowering his hands so the one rested at my waist and the other wrapped securely around me, palm splayed across my back. My skin seemed to burn under his touch, even through my dress and coat, but I only arched into him further, my own hands having moved to cup his face at some point.

Surprisingly, it was Fergus who broke the kiss. However, his expression told me he severely regretted it.

"Ye cannae be so good at kissing. Ye'll be the death of me, Ellen," he breathed.

I enjoyed the effect I so clearly had on him too much for my own good.

"Suppose I'll just have to stay over here, then, until the weather clears."

I stepped back so I was now pressed against the glass of the shop's window, as far as the small nook would allow.

I couldn't identify the expression that took over Fergus' face. Something reminiscent of a wolf who'd managed to corner his prey with no escape. My heart beat wildly in my chest; I was happy to be the rabbit he'd captured. With one solid step, he was back in my space, successfully trapping me. My breathing hitched as I peered up at him, awaiting his next move.

"Christ. Who am I kidding? Ye've been the death of me since the moment I met ye."

And then he kissed me in such a devastating way, I thought I might actually die from the pleasure.

Chapter 16

Ellen

"Miss McLean!"

I turned to find Dr. MacTavish waving me down as he dodged between students.

"Could I speak to you in my office?"

Even though it was Dr. MacTavish, a professor I had—what I believed to be—mutual respect for, I still found myself breaking out in a cold sweat. I had to wonder if I'd ever grow out of that reaction to being called in by a superior. Would I be working in a research facility and have my heart start racing whenever my boss asked to speak to me?

Trying to ignore the anxious pit in my stomach, I did my best to smile at him, hoping it didn't come out more of a grimace. "Of course."

Without another word, he turned the corner, leaving me to follow behind. I walked stiffly, trying to talk some sense into my body so it would calm down. When we reached his office, he gestured to one of the chairs and then closed the door behind us. I carefully set my stack of textbooks on the floor next to my feet, grateful to be disburdened.

"I won't keep you long," Dr. MacTavish promised as he took a seat behind his desk. The elderly man was practically vibrating. "A colleague of mine in London reached out to inform me they are making advances in a study of organ transplantation. Immunosuppressant drugs are being developed and having a positive effect on the results of transplants. He's invited me to help with his research."

"That sounds like quite the opportunity, Dr. MacTavish."

"It is. And I'd like you to join me as a research assistant."

I just stared at him for a moment, my brain trying to process his words and what they meant. "Me?"

Dr. MacTavish just beamed at me, "You're my best student, and I know how passionate you are about medical research. You said it yourself; this is quite the opportunity and it would open so many doors for you."

He was right. Joining him would allow me to network with those in the field I wanted to enter once I had my degree. I'd get first-hand experiences I could reference in interviews, and have professionals who could vouch for me. It'd give me an upper hand in a process I would already be starting off with a disadvantage.

"So, I would be joining you in London," I clarified.

"Yes. We'd begin in June and continue through the summer. While the research may run into the fall, I only promised until the start of next school year," he explained. "A flat would be provided for you, rent covered, so you would have your own space while we're there."

This was an opportunity I simply could not pass up. Dr. MacTavish had said it himself; this would open up so many doors for me and, as a woman, I unfortunately needed as many opened as possible. It was far easier than having to beat them down myself.

"I accept your offer."

"Wonderful," he smiled radiantly. "I'll gather all the necessary information and make sure to pass it along to you as soon as possible."

He stood then, so I gathered up my books and stood as well. Stepping around his desk, he held out his hand.

"I am very much looking forward to working with you, Miss McLean."

I was surprised to feel a flush rise to my cheeks. Flattery rarely made me flustered—unless it was from Fergus. But this was not a flush of embarrassment; it was a flush of pride. A scholar of high standing with extensive experience in the medical field was excited to work with *me*. I eagerly took his hand and shook it.

My eyes locked on Dr. MacTavish's, so he knew how genuine I was in my gratitude. "I look forward to it as well. Thank ye for thinking of me."

He bowed his head slightly and then held the door open for me. I almost laughed at the symbolism.

My mind was so occupied with Dr. MacTavish's offer that I hardly took any notes during my final lecture and made my way to Masson Hall on autopilot. I was bursting to tell someone, and all but rushed to the common area to call my parents.

"Ellen? But it's no even Saturday night. Is everything alright?" Mam fussed.

"I'm fine. More than fine, actually," I quickly assured her. "Is Da home? Ye'll both want to hear this."

There was a scuffling noise as she most likely held the phone against her shoulder, but I could still hear her shouting my father's name. Then her voice came back loud and clear.

"We're both here now."

"Hello, dearie," Da greeted. "Your mam says ye have news of some sort?"

There would be no easing them into this. I needed to say it and say it now.

"Dr. MacTavish invited me to join him in London as his research assistant for a study on organ transplants." The line was silent, my parents most likely as stunned as I had been, so I continued on. "It'll start in June and they'll provide me with a flat.

Can you believe it? My own flat!"

No closet-sized dorm room with too much furniture. No irritating flatmates that blatantly disregarded me and my space. My own place all to myself.

"So ye'll be conducting research with professionals? Oh, Ellen! That is absolutely wonderful!" Mam cheered.

"We're proud of ye, Ellen. That's a high honor and ye deserve every bit of it. Ye work so hard," Da added.

"And you're so passionate! They'll absolutely adore ye."

"It's all thanks to the both of ye." I suddenly felt myself getting teary-eyed and had to swallow the lump in my throat before I could continue. "Ye've always encouraged me to pursue my interests, even if they weren't the most conventional."

Mam laughed gently. "Ye ken we dinna care about conventional. We just want ye to succeed in whatever you're passionate about. That's what's most important."

I knew I had lucked out with my parents. They'd created a safe place for me and my brothers to be our authentic selves. Even if Mam had been gone the first few years of my life, she'd more than made up for it since then, fanning the flames of my passion for medicine and guiding me through the rough terrain of being a woman in the medical field.

"I love ye," I blurted.

"Love ye, too," Mam murmured.

"More than all the heather on the hills," Da cooed, and once again, I was a little girl being tucked into bed for the night.

We bid each other goodbye and I hung up the receiver, only to pick it back up and dial Fergus' number. As the phone rang, I smiled at the realization that I had someone special—outside of my family—to share good news with.

"Hullo?"

My smile grew, and my heart-rate picked up at the mere sound of his voice. "Hi, it's Ellen. Are ye busy?"

"Not at all," he answered quickly.

"In that case, would ye like to go somewhere? I've got something to tell ye and I want to do it in person."

"Of course. I'll be right over to get ye."

Chapter 17

Fergus

My heart did a little flip in my chest when I spotted Ellen waiting for me, leaning against the railing of the stairs. Her dark locks swirled around her in the spring breeze, rays of the lowering sun making it look more of a richer brown than usual.

We hadn't seen each other since our date. She hadn't been in the library at all this week, or at least not at the same time as me. It had only been a few days, but I was anxious to be near her. I'd thought about our kiss, or rather kisses, more times than I could count. Often finding myself thinking of the feel of her lips on mine instead of attending to the work in front of me. Never had I struggled so much with focusing on my studies.

And proper sleep? Forget about it. I'd lie in bed creating lists of possible dates we could go on, wondering if it was something Ellen would enjoy. When I did sleep, I dreamt of her more often than not. Nothing too terribly detailed—I'd never been one for very vivid dreams. Usually, it was those captivating eyes of hers I fantasized about. I'd happily drown in them any day.

When she spotted my car, she practically skipped down the rest of the stairs. I pulled along the curb and let the car idle as I climbed out to meet her.

I reached out to catch Ellen by her waist when she was near enough. She braced her hands on my upper arms and she looked up at me.

"Hi," she breathed out, her smile absolutely radiant.

"Hullo." The depth of my voice startled me, so I tried to subtly clear my throat. The things this woman did to me. "Are ye ready, then?"

She nodded, lips pressed together, but it did nothing to hide her grin. I desperately wished she wasn't hiding her lips so I could kiss them. I must have been staring, because Ellen let out a light laugh and then leaned up to press her lips to mine instead.

I allowed my arms to slip further around her and bring her close.

"Hi," I murmured against her mouth.

She giggled like I'd heard her do that night at the dance hall. Except this time, I was the cause of the giggle and I was absolutely elated.

"Ye already said that."

"Aye, I did. But I wanted to say it again." I stole one more kiss from her before letting her go so I could open the passenger door.

The moment Ellen had hung up our call, I knew where I wanted to take her. While St. Margaret's Loch was a man-made loch, it was still stunning with the ruins of St. Anthony's Chapel looking down from the hill above. If evening traffic continued to work in my favor, we'd be there just in time to watch the sun set. The Scottish weather was at least playing nice, not a drop of rain the entire day, and the sun shining brightly to warm us all up.

I found a spot to pull over within walking distance of the loch. Before continuing around to the passenger side, I stopped to retrieve an old, tartan blanket from the backseat. From the moment I started driving, my mother had insisted I carry a blanket in the car in case I got stuck on the side of the road in bad weather. While I'd yet to use the blanket for that purpose, it came in handy now.

With the perfectly worn fabric draped over my arm, I walked around the back of the car so I could open Ellen's door. Instead, I found her standing on the curb with a knowing smile on her face.

"Couldna wait just two seconds, could ye?" I teased.

She merely shrugged in a 'what-can-you-do' way, but her smile gave away how pleased she was with herself. In another attempt at being a gentleman, I held my free arm out in offering, and thankfully, she took it. I led her down the winding path, gravel crunching underneath our feet as we made our way to the edge of St. Margaret's Loch.

There were a few other visitors dotted along the shore, but it seemed as if most of them were packing up so they'd be ready to leave once the sun had set.

"How about here? We'll have a great view of the sun setting behind St. Anthony's." I pointed towards the ruins.

Ellen followed my gesture. "Looks perfect to me," she agreed.

We worked together to spread out the blanket and then climbed on. She sat close enough that her shoulder brushed against my side, and I had to bite back a ridiculous grin. Her hand was mere centimeters from mine now, and the electricity jumping between us was driving me mad in the best way possible. Like magnets, my pinky found hers, hooking over the slender digit.

"Can ye believe I've never been here before?" Ellen mused. "I've lived here almost three years now and never managed to make it very far from campus."

"Really?"

I didn't mean to sound so shocked, but I must have based on her laugh.

"Yes, really." She shrugged, but the playfulness in her expression had dimmed considerably. "It's no like I had many friends to explore with."

I stroked my pinky along hers, bringing her attention back to me. "Ye've got me now. And Freya and Doug, too. We can go wherever ye want. We could even explore outside of Edinburgh."

Her smile was shy as she looked up at me from under her dark lashes. "I may take you up on that," she replied, her voice quiet.

I adjusted on the blanket so I faced her more. "So, what's this news ye wanted to share? I've been patiently waiting, but I dinna think I can wait anymore," I chuckled.

She straightened. "Dr. MacTavish invited me to London to be his assistant for a study they are conducting on organ transplantation. Fergus, it's...*amazing* the advances they're making."

The world seemed to spin around me. I could see her lips moving excitedly, but the words weren't processing anymore, her voice muffled by the blood suddenly pulsing in my ears. The feel of her hand on my shoulder jolted me back into the moment.

"Fergus?"

"How...how long?" I stammered.

"I'd leave at the beginning of June and then return for the fall semester."

I felt sick. How could this be happening? We'd just started going steady, and now she was leaving me? Did she even see it as going steady, or was I completely alone in my feelings for her? Had I been fooling myself this whole time? No, those kisses meant something. Didn't they?

"Fergus," her voice was sterner this time, and her grip firmer. "*Breathe.*"

I forced myself to look at her, however the sight of those loch blue eyes had me reeling all over again.

What if I never saw them again?

"Yes." I cleared my throat. "Yes. I'm alright."

I nodded my head once, but she didn't seem convinced. It sure didn't convince me.

Ellen at least had the decency to look somewhat ashamed. "I'm sorry. I–when I accepted, I didn't think–"

"Ye didna think about me," I finished.

She might as well have punched me right in the gut. I'd actually prefer that at the moment.

"No! I did." She let out a frustrated huff.

What if she never came back? They'd realize how gifted she was and hire her on to the London research team for good. Honestly, they'd be stupid not to.

"What do we do?" I finally managed. "End it here?"

Her hand found mine once more, clinging to it almost desperately. Or at least that's what I told myself. "No. I dinna want to do that."

"So ye want me to just wait here in the chance ye come back for me, then, is it?" I hated how bitter I sounded.

"I could never ask that of ye."

There was no more fight in her voice, and I'd be

lying if I said I didn't notice the tears in the corners of her gorgeous eyes. The fight had left me as well. I leaned forward to press my forehead to hers, not able to stand the sight of her so torn.

"And I could never ask ye to turn down such an opportunity," I sighed.

She moved to cup my neck, keeping me in place even though I had no desire to move anytime soon. I reached up to gently wrap my fingers around her wrist so she couldn't move away either. Now I was the one clinging desperately to her. I wasn't ready to let go of what we had. So, we stayed there, our breathing eventually syncing and her pulse calming underneath my thumb.

"It's settled, then. You don't ask me to stay and I don't ask ye to wait," she decided.

"We take it day by day," I offered.

I watched as her red lips pressed together. Before I knew it, I was tilting my head just enough so I could pry her lips apart with my own, kissing her gently and slowly. This wasn't like the kisses on our first date; eager and exploring. No, this one was more reverent. If my time with her was limited, I'd better make the most of it.

When we pulled apart, Ellen burrowed herself

completely into my side, head on my shoulder, and face nuzzled into my neck. We'd missed the sunset and the sky was now pink and purple as the last light fought to stay for just a few minutes more.

"Tell me again about the study," I requested. "I cannae promise to ken what you're talking about, but I want to hear it."

I was relieved to hear her laugh, even if it was small. We sat there, alone on the shore of the loch, and I listened intently as she talked.

Chapter 18

Ellen

March

"Izik is not a word, Dougie! Fergus. Get the dictionary and check him," Freya fussed.

"It's just another spelling for Isaac," Doug objected.

I never knew a game of Scrabble to be so intense, but this group was proving me wrong. Freya was analytical of every word placed down and made sure we were all following the rules; Doug was just doing whatever he could to entertain Freya and piss off Fergus; and Fergus was absolutely ruthless, constantly putting down high-scoring words. How he knew so many terms containing difficult letters like Z and X was beyond me.

The job of keeping score had fallen to me once Doug realized I could add up numbers as quick as they were putting down the tiles. While they were all linguistically inclined—and therefore scoring painfully higher than me—I was at least somewhat useful thanks to my mathematical skills.

Fergus eyed his best mate. "Ye ken well it isna a word. Take your pieces back."

"Och, you're no fun," Doug groaned, but the small curve of his lips belied him.

He removed his tiles from the board and then sat back with a huff, arms crossed as he eyed his rack to decide which letters to trade out. It seemed the switch helped enough that he was able to make a word that did actually exist, though the score wasn't much to boast about.

It was Fergus' turn, and I was hesitant to see what he'd put down. He was already well in the lead and we were all losing hope of ever catching up. Now it was mostly a competition to see who could get second.

Fergus slapped two tiles onto the board, and I leaned forward to get a better look at the points.

"Zek?" Now it was my turn to eye my lad questionably.

My lad. That was an odd thing to think. It'd been so long since I'd had a man to call my own. I shivered at the memory of the only other relationship I'd been in. It had ended when I told him about my acceptance into the university, and he laughed in my face. *Why would ye need to go to uni? Do ye no ken how to cook and clean a house?*

Fergus' smug voice broke me from my thoughts. "A zek is an inmate in a Soviet labor camp."

Doug sunk even further down in his chair, shooting daggers at his friend as he pouted. "I'm never tellin' ye my interesting facts ever again."

"Aye, I'll believe it when I see it. You're a historian. Ye love to talk about the past," Fergus quipped.

Freya groaned next to me, rolling her eyes. "Don't I know it!"

Doug lightly knocked his knee against hers.

With the word confirmed, I added the points to his score. "Alright. Then that puts Fergus at two hundred seventy-three."

I was quite shocked to find his lips turned down as he looked over the board.

"That's good, isn't it?" I ventured.

Doug chuckled. "That's actually quite low for Fergus here. He's normally in the three hundreds by now."

"Oh."

Fergus waved his hand dismissively as he lounged back, trying to appear at ease and not doing a very good job of it. I could still see the clenched muscles of his jaw.

"Usually, that's with less players. Four players means less space to create larger words."

I let out a sigh and pushed back from the table. "I need some tea. Anyone else?"

"And some biscuits?" Doug smiled hopefully.

I hadn't spent much time in the lads' kitchen, but figured I'd be able to find everything. Freya must have noticed my hesitation because she stood as well.

"I'll help you."

I smiled gratefully and then turned my attention to the lads, eyeing both of them. "No cheating."

Doug raised his hands defensively, giving me his most innocent look, while Fergus just smiled up at me.

"It's not like we could read your chicken scratch

anyways," he teased.

I just scrunched my nose at him, which made him laugh, and what a beautiful sound it was.

I'd barely stepped through the door into the kitchen when Freya gently grabbed my elbow and guided me to the opposite side near the refrigerator. The poor thing made a terrible noise as if it took all of its effort just to keep its contents below room temperature. It also covered the sound of our voices so the lads wouldn't hear us, which seemed to be exactly Freya's intention.

"I knew it!" she squeaked. Her grin was so big, it might've split her face.

"I think we all kent Doug was making up that word to try and get the high points from 'Z'."

Freya's eyes rolled, an expression typically reserved for Doug, and then nudged my arm. "No! You and Fergus."

"What about us?" I continued to play dumb.

"I knew you'd make a great couple. I told you so at the house party, but you told me you weren't looking for a relationship. Now look at you." She raised her brows, a smug smile on her lips.

I wasn't one for admitting I was wrong. Even though I loved and trusted Freya, I still found it hard to get the words out. They were caught in my throat, resisting exposure, and it felt as if I had to physically force them out.

"Okay, you were right."

Freya just let out another squeak. "Oh, you two are utterly adorable! I've never seen him so distracted during a game of Scrabble."

"What are ye talking about? He's destroying us all."

She shook her head. "This is Fergus going easy. Usually, he's laser-focused and already three steps ahead of Doug, but not tonight. He keeps looking at you," she smiled smugly.

Those darn butterflies began to flutter in my stomach, and I crossed my arms as if to keep them inside where no one could see. I wasn't used to someone making me feel this way; all flushed and giddy. The man wasn't even in the room with me, and he was making me flustered at the mere mention of him.

"I don't know what he's going to do when you're off in London," Freya mused absently.

The butterflies' wings wilted. Even though he'd been more than supportive of me going, I felt guilty for leaving him here when we'd just started going steady.

The kitchen door swung open, and we both turned to find Fergus standing in the doorway, a skeptical expression on his face as his eyes darted between the two of us.

"I'm interrupting, aren't I?" His gaze shifted to the kettle, which was definitely not on the burner. "And there is no tea, is there?"

He actually looked quite disappointed. Enough that I found myself moving to the stove.

"I'll get it started now," I assured him.

The burner switched on with a satisfying click and *whoosh*. I was so focused on filling the kettle, I didn't notice Freya slipping out of the kitchen. But then I felt a touch at the small of my back that was far too intimate to be anyone other than Fergus, even for the overly affectionate Freya. Sure enough, it was his smile that greeted me when I turned my head. I found myself suddenly fixated on the tiny dimple at the apple of his cheek, and overfilled the kettle.

Fergus darted back to avoid the spill before quickly reaching to turn off the faucet. "Whoa there. Are ye sure ye ken how to make tea?" he chuckled, clearly amused at my fumbling.

"Yes," I huffed, turning away so he wouldn't see

my now pink cheeks. "You just...distracted me."

Without looking at him, I knew he now wore the smuggest expression. When we'd first met, that look would have irked me to no end, but now I found it quite winsome. What had this man done to me?

I at least managed to place the kettle on the burner with no further incident and went to retrieve four tea cups when it dawned on me that I didn't know where they were located. As if reading my mind, Fergus reached around me to open the cabinet to my left.

"We dinna have a set, exactly. More of a hodgepodge of cups we've collected or been gifted over the years."

I took in the precarious stacks of cups ranging from intricate designs with gold trim to more understated cups of a single color. While it was quite fitting for Doug's personality, it seemed like something that would make the meticulous Fergus Morgan itch.

"I honestly cannae believe ye allow this," I teased him.

He took a deep breath, filling his chest so the fabric of his sweater stretched tight across it. "I didna say I liked it."

His body sank back into the counter as he gave a shrug, bracing his hands on the edge of the wood. I carefully brought down the four topmost cups and set them out on the counter.

"I had to make some compromises living with Doug. He's allowed to keep his room in whatever state he pleases, so long as the living room is tidy. Fridge stays properly organized and Doug can have his mismatched dishware and cutlery."

"How do ye even manage with *that* much disorder?"

His lips curled into a smirk as he peered at me from the corner of his eyes. "I'm no that bad."

I leveled him with a look, head dipped and eyebrows raised high. The expression made him laugh.

"Okay, okay. I may have a slight problem," he relented.

I knew well how it felt to have your unique traits treated as odd or abnormal, and I never wanted to make Fergus feel that way, so I reached out and took his hand in mine.

"It's what makes ye, you. Besides,"—I shrugged—"I could use a little more order in my life."

His laugh this time was more of a snort, and it

just made me laugh, too. I knew that was an understatement; I was terrible at organizing anything. My space reflected the chaos inside of my brain, thoughts and items everywhere.

Fergus gave my hand a tug, pulling me towards him. His free hand went to my waist as he bent his head down to press a kiss to my forehead.

"I love that chaotic brain of yours," he murmured, lips still brushing my skin.

That cleared the chaos up right away, my mind completely wiped of any thoughts that didn't revolve around this man and his touch. At some point, my own unoccupied hand had found his sweater and clutched at the worn knit, keeping myself tethered to the here and now.

I managed to tilt my head up enough to meet his gaze, his eyes warm despite their blue hues. Like a moth to a flame, I found myself closing the space between us.

Wheeeeeeeee!

We jumped at the shrill sound of the kettle and I mentally cursed the damn thing for its interruption. Fergus let go of my hand to move it off the burner. I had begun to settle back down onto my feet when I suddenly found myself wrapped in his embrace and his lips on mine.

"The tea can wait."

The gruff tone of his voice sent shockwaves through my body, and I desperately clung to him as I kissed him back. Every kiss we'd shared felt as if I were being lit on fire, and every bit of oxygen I managed to steal from him just fanned the flames.

Who's to say how long we stood there, practically devouring each other, before the kitchen door swung open.

"How about that tea?" Doug's voice rang out, the mocking tone evident.

Fergus' lips left mine. "Bugger off," he muttered.

His mouth was a striking color of pink that matched the blush in his cheeks. He looked thoroughly kissed. I must've looked similar as we both burst into giggles and grins.

How would I ever get enough of him?

Chapter 19

Fergus

April

"Fancy meeting you here."

I jumped, yanked out of my hyper-focused editing of my manuscript. Ellen giggled at my reaction, but did her best to muffle the sound behind her hand to keep from drawing the attention of the librarian. I peeked around to make sure we didn't have an audience before I tugged on her hand to remove it from her mouth and pull her down to my level so I could kiss her. She made the most endearing noise of surprise.

"You're a wee devil sometimes, ye ken? Sneaking

up on me in a library," I muttered.

She stood up straight, that ornery smile still on her face despite my hopes of wiping it off.

"Gotta keep ye on your toes," she winked before sliding into the seat next to me.

I shifted over my things as she unpacked her bag, leaving plenty of space between. It baffled me how many textbooks she carried around. They weren't light reading, and she was a petite lass, but knowing Ellen, she'd never complain or let on how heavy the load was.

My arm draped across the back of her chair as I looked over at her open notebook. "What are ye working on?"

"I've been trying to get some research done before London. Previous attempts at transplantation, where it went wrong and what they think went right. I've spent a lot of time focusing on the research of Dr. Murray."

She shifted around the books in front of her— conscious to keep them in her space—until she found the right one.

"He was the first to conduct a successful kidney transplant just ten years ago, but he'd been studying the possibilities for years. Practically everyone else had given up, saying the body would always reject the donation."

The fire within her was blazing, and I smiled at the sight of it. Her passion and brains were so attractive to me. I was convinced there wasn't another woman like her.

"But he proved them wrong. Then, in fifty-nine, he performed the first successful allograft."

"Layman's terms, my dear," I chuckled.

She smiled sheepishly at me as if she just now realized who she was speaking to. "Sorry. An allograft is a donation from a non-identical donor."

"Understood. Continue."

"The research we'll be doing is on immunosuppressants and how they affect the success rate of transplants between non-identical donors. The idea being they will keep the body from attacking the donated organ no matter who it came from."

I sat back and blew a breath out through my lips as I looked over my own work. My manuscript was in its last editing phases before I was ready to begin querying it. Then that was a process in and of itself.

"Well...your work is much more life-changing than mine," I chuckled.

Ellen gave my leg a solid nudge with her own. "Now don't go saying that. Your book will have an impact on people. I ken it did on my mam."

I leveled her with a look. "She hasn't even read it yet."

"No, but she willna stop raving about ye interviewing her and how her stories are going to be in a novel."

"If it gets published."

"When."

Ellen's look was severe, just daring me to continue to argue with her. I knew better than that.

"Aye," I agreed. "*When* it gets published and becomes a bestseller."

"Better," she sniffed.

Between being so immersed in my edits and the comforting presence of Ellen grinding away beside me, I'd lost track of how much time I'd spent in the library. I'd stayed nearly twenty minutes over my usual limit of three hours.

Normally, I would have been panicking over the alteration in my routine, but currently, I found myself unable to fathom moving. Ellen and I had barely a month before she left for London and with nothing else demanding my time, it'd be foolish to walk away from her. It wasn't like anything was waiting for me at home. Doug would most likely be out with Freya, and I would simply continue to edit my novel in my bedroom or at the kitchen table.

I must've drawn Ellen's attention in some way, because she checked her own timepiece before looking at me with wide eyes. "Your routine."

"Aye," I chuckled, leaning in close. "Ye've made me stay past my allotted time."

"*I* made ye? I did no such thing."

"Oh, so ye want me to leave then?"

She snatched my hand before I could even sit fully upright. "No. Stay."

Her eyes were earnest as she waited for my next move, and I happily slipped back into their depths, drifting closer to her once more.

"I will," I promised. My stomach let out a gurgle then, causing us both to laugh. "Would ye mind terribly if I left just long enough to get us food?"

"She'd kill ye if ye brought food into the library."

Ellen glanced over my shoulder in the direction of the librarian's desk as if she'd conjure the old biddy.

"I'll sneak it past her in my satchel. If you dinna tell, I won't."

She nibbled thoughtfully on her bottom lip, clearly debating the risks versus the rewards.

"How about a bridie?" I offered enticingly. The meat pastry was meant to be eaten with your hands and wouldn't make a mess if we were careful.

"Can I get two?"

I had to keep myself from laughing, knowing it'd just embarrass her, and simply nodded instead.

"Absolutely. As many as ye want." Standing, I quietly pushed in my chair and then bent to place a kiss to her temple. "I'll be right back."

She smiled up at me. "Thank ye, Fergus."

There was a pub not too far off campus from the library, and it was late enough that I had missed the supper rush. The fact I was taking the food to go helped as well. Within minutes, I had four freshly-baked bridies secured in my satchel. The leather would probably hold onto the meat and onion smell for a while, but it was worth it. My stomach was growling something vicious by the time I made it back to the library. I could only hope the scent would stay contained long enough for me to make it to Ellen.

Playing it casual, I sent the librarian a polite smile as I passed, like I always did—even if I never received a smile in return. She simply glanced at me over the rim of her spectacles before returning to her records.

Ellen looked up as soon as I turned the corner, an eager smile on her face.

"Please tell me ye didna smell them all the way over here," I worried.

She laughed and shook her head. "No. I ken your footsteps."

With a quick check of our surroundings, I retrieved the to-go bag and passed it to Ellen under the table.

"Fergus Morgan, you are a saint," she practically groaned.

Despite her obvious hunger, she still passed me a bridie first before claiming one for herself. We tried to be as subtle as possible. Being quick wasn't a concern, though. All four bridies were scarfed down in record time.

"I might have been hungrier than I thought," Ellen laughed sheepishly.

Crumpling the empty paper bag, I secured it in my satchel once more, making a mental note to get rid of it at home to minimize the stench.

"How much more do ye think you're going to do?" I asked, nodding towards the clutter of papers and books in front of her.

She'd completely encroached on my space while I was gone, but I had decided to call it good for today anyway. The bridies had left me stuffed and unmotivated. Ellen, however, only looked rejuvenated.

"Too much," she shook her head. "I'll probably stay until close, but dinna feel like ye have to stay with me."

I shrugged, "I want to."

Her smile was soft as she reached for my hand. I kept hold of it even as I retrieved a novel from my bag to read.

And so we sat there, my thumb absently stroking over the back of her hand as she continued her research. Physically connected even as our minds were in separate worlds.

Chapter 20

Fergus

May

Doug had chosen Dunbar's Close as the location for his proposal to Freya. The small garden was tucked away behind the buildings lining the Royal Mile, accessible only through an alleyway. Nestled next to the church wall, the parterres bloomed with brightly colored flowers this time of year, and the shrubbery provided the perfect hideout for myself and Ellen. Doug had entrusted me with his camera to capture the moment. Each thump of the camera against my chest as we trekked up the hill reminded me of how important my job was. A proposal was a—

hopefully—once-in-a-lifetime event, and I would be solely responsible for preserving that memory in a physical photograph.

Ellen's hand slipped into mine, and I looked down to find her smiling gently at me. "Breathe, Fergus."

"I am."

She laughed. "If you mean hyperventilating, then yes." She stroked her thumb soothingly along the back of my hand. "Everything will turn out fine."

The muscles in my shoulders and neck relaxed at her reassurances. We continued on until we reached the close and stepped off the main road. The further we went through the tunnel, the more hushed the city sounds grew. It felt like a completely different world within the close. I led Ellen to the spot Doug and I had agreed upon. On this side of the garden were several compartments where a holly stood in the middle, surrounded by hedges on three sides. It was the perfect nook for us to hide in.

Murmured voices drifted towards us, but they didn't belong to Doug or Freya. In the lower section of the garden, a couple had taken residence in the shade of a tree.

"Damnit," I muttered.

It didn't seem as if they were going anywhere anytime soon, cuddled up as they were on the wood bench.

"I'll get rid of them," Ellen offered, already striding towards the couple.

"Be nice about it!" I called after her.

She spun on her heel, the gravel crunching beneath the sole of her shoe, and looked at me aghast. "Me? Rude?"

I lifted an eyebrow. As if I didn't know her.

She laughed and playfully rolled her eyes. "Fine, fine. I'll be polite."

I watched her just to be sure and figured she'd been true to her word when the couple smiled apologetically and hurried down the path, nodding at me as they passed. With the minor inconvenience handled, I double-checked the lighting of the camera. Doug had talked me through it, but I wasn't completely confident.

I lifted the camera up and peered through the viewfinder, adjusting the focus onto Ellen as she strode back to me with a satisfied grin. Figuring Doug wouldn't mind me using one frame, I snapped a picture of her. Her brows crinkled in the middle when she heard the click of the camera.

"What are ye doing? You're gonna use up the film before they even get here," she lightly scolded.

I shrugged as I lowered the camera, "I was doing a test shot."

She tried not to smile, but it seemed to be a losing fight. "Did ye at least get the settings right?"

"I think so."

"Here." Ellen moved to stand by my side. "Let me see."

Without removing the neck strap, I held the camera out for her. She leaned in to peer at what Doug had called the light meter, glanced up at the cloudy sky above us, and then began to make adjustments.

"It's overcast, so you need an aperture of f/8 and shutter speed of one hundredth of a second."

It all sounded like nonsense to me; numbers and letters jumbled together with jargon I was unfamiliar with. Ellen confidently passed the camera back to me, a bemused expression on her beautiful face when she found me staring at her.

"What? That's what Doug told ye to do."

"And ye remembered all that?"

She just shrugged as if it were simple, and to her brilliant mind, it probably was. I opened my mouth to compliment her when I heard Freya's distinct accent floating down the alleyway, the bricks amplifying her voice. When it came to fight or flight instinct, I was apparently someone who froze. My feet might as well have been trapped in a bog, unmoving, while my eyes frantically scanned the area for a place to hide. If Freya saw Ellen and I, she'd surely be suspicious.

Ellen shoved me backwards into the alcove, and my heel caught on a root, sending me tumbling back into the hedges. She tried to remedy the situation by grabbing my arm in an attempt to catch me, but I greatly outweighed her, and the effort only resulted in her falling with me. Several branches cracked under our weight, but for the most part, the sturdy hedge held us up. I was not keen on the particular offshoot stabbing just under my left shoulder blade, though.

"What was that?" Freya gasped.

Ellen slapped a hand over my mouth, and I frowned at her, only to realize she couldn't even see it. As if I would actually respond to Freya.

"Probably a street cat chasing its prey," Doug explained easily, but I could hear the touch of nerves in his voice.

As much as I loved having Ellen in my arms, I wouldn't be able to get a picture of Doug's proposal in this position. Especially not with the camera hanging at my side and my hands more concerned with keeping Ellen steady. So, I planted my hands on her waist and pushed her up until she was properly standing. Then she assisted with removing me from the hedge's clutch.

I could hear Doug and Freya's footsteps nearing. We'd planned for him to take her to one of the benches amongst the flower beds and get on one knee there. I snuck to the edge of the bush, camera ready in my hands. Thank God I'd had the neck strap on or Doug would have killed me if I'd broken his camera in my fall.

"Why don't we sit here?" I heard Doug suggest.

Lifting the camera up once more, I took the tiniest peek around the shrubbery through the viewfinder. Freya had sat down on the stone bench, but Doug was still standing, his hands shoved deep in his pockets.

"Freya," he started. I could practically see the nerves rolling off of him all the way over here.

Ellen placed her hand on my back to keep herself balanced while peeking around the bush as well. I held an arm out to stop her from leaning too far. Not that I had to worry; Freya's eyes were locked on Doug, her attention completely on him. She gasped when he knelt down, and I let go of Ellen to snap a picture of Freya's expression.

"I'm sure I've told ye before that I kent early on I wanted to marry ye. It's no something I've kept a secret. But I wanted the moment to be right when I asked ye, because ye deserve to feel special and loved." He retrieved the ring from his pocket and held it out to her. I took another picture. "I'd like to spend the rest of my life making sure ye do. Freya...will ye marry me?"

Ellen gripped my arm now, her excitement palpable. My finger lingered over the shutter button.

Freya let out a watery laugh, shaking her head a little. "Of course, I'll marry you, Dougie."

Click. He slid the ring onto her finger. *Click.* Both of them stood, and Freya threw her arms around his neck to kiss him. *Click.*

"Whoooo!" Ellen cheered next to me.

Freya jerked back from Doug and looked in our direction, only to laugh once she spotted us peering around the hedge. I lowered the camera and smiled sheepishly at her.

"I should've known the two of you would have something to do with this," she teased.

We stepped out from the alcove to join them. I'd never seen my friend smile so big. Not even when he'd scored the winning goal and his football team won the championship in sixth year.

I gave him a hearty slap on the shoulder while Ellen hugged Freya. "Congratulations. I took as many pictures as I could."

Doug beamed. "Thank ye, Fergus. I appreciate all your help." He leaned close to whisper in my ear. "I'll return the favor when it's your turn."

His eyes darted back and forth between Ellen and me as he pulled away, eyebrows wiggling, and I knew my cheeks were bright red.

"Let's not rush anything," I eyed him.

Freya hugged me then. "You two were so sneaky. I didn't even know you were there."

"Ellen about gave us away, shoving me into the hedges," I muttered, smirking at Ellen over Freya's shoulder.

Freya stepped back and looked between the two of us. "That was you?"

"I didna shove him into the hedges," Ellen

protested. "I just pushed him out of sight, and he tripped into the hedges."

Freya reached forward and plucked something from Ellen's sleeve. A little sprig with bright green leaves. "And you fell with him?" she smiled knowingly.

"He pulled me."

Freya simply hummed, leaving it at that, but I could tell from her expression that this would not be the last we heard of the incident.

I clapped my hands together to redirect everyone's attention. "Shall we go celebrate?"

The night was about Doug and Freya's relationship, after all. Not mine and Ellen's. With everyone's agreement, we made our way back towards the Royal Mile, Doug and Freya leading the way.

Ellen slipped her hand into the crook of my arm and leaned against me as we walked. "I saw ye tearing up back there when Doug was giving his speech. You're quite the romantic, Fergus."

I narrowed my eyes in challenge. "What proof do ye have?"

She grinned; that beautiful, yet evil smile she wore when she knew she was right and had all the means to prove me wrong.

"I've been on a handful of dates with ye, have I no? First, there was you getting so upset, ye stormed out of the dance hall because ye saw me dancing with another man. That sounds like something out of a romance novel to me."

My jaw dropped. "I didna storm out."

Ellen made a noise in her throat, letting me know she strongly disagreed. "Face it, Fergus. Ye felt so passionately about me, ye couldna handle seeing me in another man's arms."

She wasn't wrong.

"Is that all ye have, then? Because it doesna sound like a strong argument to me."

"Hmm," she pondered. "Well, there's the date where ye made sure to pick a film I would be interested in. Our kiss in the rain. The way ye rushed over to my dormitory when I called ye. And–"

"Wait," I interrupted her, even though I'd gladly listen to her sing my praises all day. "Go back to the kiss part. What was so romantic about it?"

She let out a loud huff then, and I grinned, knowing I was getting under her skin. I wanted to hear her say it. To let me know our kiss had affected her just as much as me; that when she was in

London, she'd reminisce on it and wish I were there so we could have more.

"Get that shite-eating grin off your face."

That just made me laugh; the throw-back-your-head, belly-laugh kind. Ellen continued to glare, so I tempered my humor as quickly as I could.

"Fine, fine. *I'll* say it." I paused, making sure I had her attention, and then lowered my voice. "It was the best kiss I've ever had. Absolutely intoxicating. I would've stayed there all night with ye, rain or no."

She was quiet for a few more moments, and it felt like my heart was in my throat.

"See? A romantic."

Chapter 21

Ellen

I'd already thrown up twice this morning from nerves. There couldn't possibly be anything left in my stomach. Joining this study was the opportunity of a lifetime, but I wasn't naive. I knew it would be hard work and I would have to prove myself like I always had, even with the praise of Dr. MacTavish.

Looking in the mirror—at my very green reflection—I straightened to my full height and pushed my shoulders back.

"I am intelligent. I deserve to be there. I will open the door so others may follow."

If anything pushed me along when others doubted my abilities due to my gender, it was the knowledge that there were women like me who would benefit from me persevering. Whether they were in the medical field now or would pursue it in the future, I had to be strong for them.

In a better mindset than the one I'd woken up in, I did one last check to make sure my dorm was completely empty. While the study did not begin for another week, they'd been kind enough to allow me to move into the provided flat directly after the end of the school year. I'd managed to pack all of my things into just two suitcases, books included.

The second I stepped out of the main doors, Fergus hurried to take them from me. Then he got a good look at me and the suitcases clattered onto the pavement. Within seconds, my face was cupped between his hands.

"Oh, Ellen. Are ye alright? Ye look a bit peely-wally," he fretted.

Maybe I should have thrown on some blush before I left. I did my best to smile as reassuringly as I could. "I'm fine. Just the nerves getting to me."

He looked me over once more and then gave a small nod, slowly removing his hands and picking up my luggage again. I followed him down the stairs, lightly resting my hand on the railing just in case my shaky legs should give out on me.

"I stopped by to get ye some of Clara's scones for the trip. She's got new flavors for summer."

The familiarity of the gesture made my heart squeeze both out of affection and heartache. Who knew if there'd be a cafe in London with scones as delicious and unique as Clara's. More than that, I would miss Fergus' little surprises.

"I can't wait to try them," I smiled.

I managed to reclaim one of the suitcases so I could take hold of Fergus' free hand, tightly interlocking our fingers. The train station was conveniently—and unfortunately—only a fifteen-minute walk from campus. Not nearly enough time.

"It's only a little over three months," Fergus assured me, though it sounded as if he were saying it for himself, too.

I nodded. "I'm sure time will fly with how busy I'll be."

He looked down at me proudly. "My girl, on a medical research team."

My heart melted into a puddle. *My girl.* His confidence in me boosted my spirits significantly. He'd complimented my work ethic long before we were anywhere near romantic with each other, so I always knew he wasn't just saying it because I was his girl. He genuinely meant it, and that meant more to me than I could ever tell him.

I brought our hands up to place a kiss to his knuckles. "Medical researcher and an author," I grinned at him.

"Ah, not yet." His smile dimmed as he looked off.

I nudged his leg to get his attention again. "Ye'll hear back soon, I'm sure of it. They'd be insane not to pick up your story."

I could tell he was putting on a brave face for me, and I couldn't exactly hold it against him. I was currently doing the same.

"And I better be the first person ye call when ye find out."

He raised a brow at me, lips tilted in a crooked smile. "Oh, like how I was the first one *you* called? Pretty sure ye called your parents first."

"Okay. The person ye call after your parents," I amended.

He shrugged. "That was my plan anyway."

The train station was just up ahead, and I subconsciously slowed my steps, not ready. When would I see his face next? Those eyes, bright as sapphires, that sparkled when he was particularly amused. Lips that seemed permanently pouty except for when he was kissing me, and they curved into a pleased smile. I said I wouldn't ask him to wait, but I wished more than anything he would. I'd be waiting for him.

The scream of a train whistle brought me back to the present, and I settled my suitcase next to my feet once we reached the platform. Fergus did the same and then took my other hand in his as well before bringing them both up to his lips.

"Tuesdays and Thursdays. Eight o'clock," he confirmed, blue eyes peering over our knuckles at me.

"Eight o'clock on the dot, though I ken ye'll be waiting by the phone by seven-thirty."

He laughed, and the sound momentarily broke the tension around us. "I cannae deny it."

I took in his smile once more, committing every laugh line and dimple to memory, and then threw my arms around him as I pushed up on my toes. Fergus didn't hesitate to wrap me up in his arms, lifting me off my feet. I cupped the back of his head as we kissed, pouring everything we couldn't seem to say into it. The longing, hurt, and insecurities. Neither of us knew what lay ahead for us.

When I pulled back, the words 'I love you' sat heavy on my tongue. But it wouldn't be fair to leave him with that. Not when I wasn't sure if I'd be able to follow through.

Fergus gasped suddenly. "I almost forgot!"

He opened his satchel to pull out the scones he'd purchased and held them out to me.

"Almost got away with keeping 'em for yourself, didn't ye?" I teased.

He playfully rolled his eyes. I slipped the bag of pastries into my suitcase, and then he wrapped me up in his arms once more, his head resting so easily on top of mine.

"I'm not ready for ye to go," he confessed, words partially muffled by my hair.

Tears stung my eyes, and I was grateful he couldn't see. If I tried to speak, he'd surely hear the lump in my throat, so I simply held him tighter.

"Last boarding for London," the porter called, voice loud and clear even over the rumbling engine.

There was no time left. We shared one last kiss before I slipped out of his embrace. Fergus took a step back as I picked up both suitcases and carried them to the awaiting train. There were only a few other passengers in front of me, and then it was my turn.

A porter offered to assist with my luggage, but I politely declined. I could have sworn I heard Fergus' chuckle behind me. Ascending the stairs, I maneuvered my luggage through the doorway of the car and found an empty spot in the overhead compartment before claiming a seat.

I couldn't help but search for Fergus through the window, quickly finding his dark curls in the crowd. He wasn't where I had left him. Instead, he had moved closer to the train, possibly in hopes I would see him. He spotted me then, and the corner of his lips twitched up as he tapped his watch and mouthed 'Tuesday'. I nodded my head so he knew I understood.

"Tuesday," I confirmed.

The last thing I expected to see when I arrived in London was a man holding a sign bearing my name. I'd just assumed I would find my own way to the flat. However, after the four-hour trip, I wasn't opposed to having one task taken off my plate.

"Hullo," I greeted as I approached him, ducking my head towards the sign in his hands. "I'm Ellen McLean."

He shifted the sign to one hand and held out the other to me. "Ah. Dr. MacTavish's secretary. I'm Richard Cross. Pleasure to meet you."

My teeth ground together, but I did my best to look as pleasant as possible when I corrected him, setting down my suitcase long enough to shake his hand. "Actually, I'm his assistant. I study biomedical research at the University of Edinburgh."

"A student, then?" He gave me a once-over, and I was torn between wanting to crawl out of my skin and wanting to slap him for being so bold.

"Yes. Just finished my third year. I take it you are here to chauffeur me to my accommodations. How kind of them. I do hope they tip you well." I gave him a sickeningly sweet smile.

I had to focus on my words to make sure I didn't let my Highland accent slip through. Usually, I didn't mind it, but when a bigot like the one in front of me thought he was superior due to his nationality and gender, I wasn't going to give them anything else to use against me.

My alluding to him being the help at least seemed to ruffle his feathers.

He cleared his throat. "I'm actually one of the research associates. I'm an epidemiologist," he clarified. "They wouldn't have a lady such as yourself traveling through London on her own, and I happen to live near the flat they've provided you."

Richard made a move to take my suitcases from me, but I sidestepped around him and began walking to the exit, leaving him no choice but to catch up with me. He managed to take the lead by the time we reached the street, gesturing with his arm to the left as he tipped his head in that direction.

"The car is just there."

I took it upon myself to load my suitcases when he opened the boot. Richard's car smelled fresh, as if he'd just driven it out of the lot, and was the tidiest vehicle I think I'd ever seen. Not a single speck of dust on the dashboard, and the chrome so polished I could clearly see my reflection in it. I'd thought Fergus was fairly anal, but Richard had him beat.

"Would you like to take the scenic route?" he offered once he'd settled in behind the wheel.

This was my first visit to London, and while I was

eager to see the city, the less time I spent with Richard, the better.

"That's alright. I'd rather get settled into my flat as soon as possible," I declined.

He simply nodded before starting the engine, and I was grateful he wouldn't push conversation. I wasn't up for talking at the moment and definitely not with him. Being belittled was not one of my goals today.

As we drove, I was hit with a sudden pang of longing. Had Fergus been with me, I would have happily spent the rest of the day out and about. We could go to Buckingham Palace and maybe enjoy a picnic in Hyde Park. My friends had just gotten me off campus to explore Edinburgh after all these years, and now I was back to square one; a stranger in a new city and no one to see it with.

You have Dr. MacTavish, I reminded myself. But playing tourist with my elderly professor sounded pretty pathetic in my opinion.

I was determined not to repeat the mistakes I'd made when first moving to Edinburgh. Even if I did it alone, I'd make sure I spent whatever free time I had somewhere other than the couch in my flat. After all, I'd need something interesting to tell my family and Fergus when I called. While I knew any of them would let me prattle on about the research, outside of my mother, they had little to no knowledge of what it all meant.

Richard pulled to a stop in front of a red brick building and then reached into the glove compartment to retrieve an envelope.

"The key to the building is the square one. The other is to your flat," he explained. "Slip of paper should tell you which one is yours."

Then he climbed out of the car to open the boot. I kept a tight hold of the envelope as I removed both of my suitcases and then stepped onto the curb.

"Thank you for the ride, Mr. Cross."

He dipped his head. "Suppose I'll see you soon, then, Miss McLean."

The boot slammed shut behind me as I made my way to the building. It turned out I was only on the third floor, but that didn't stop my thighs from burning on the last flight.

The flat was triple the size of my dorm in Edinburgh, and while the provided furniture was nothing to write home about, I couldn't be more elated. All of this space was mine and mine alone. No bothersome flatmate or obnoxious brothers to share it with.

I wandered into the kitchen next and noticed the phone next to the refrigerator. No more making calls from the common area with girls eavesdropping on my conversation, either.

I'd have to make a trip for groceries today. Just at the thought of it, my stomach rumbled irritably, reminding me that the only thing in it were the scones Fergus had gifted me. While they had been unspeakably delicious, they had failed to fill me up. In hindsight, I should have packed my own food to tide me over on the trip, but I had been a bit busy panicking this morning. And after spending several hours with my head in the toilet, food had been the last thing on my mind.

I made sure I had both keys before I locked up the flat behind me and made my way back downstairs. I didn't even think about the fact that I had no idea which direction to go.

"Well...I suppose it's called an adventure for a reason."

Chapter 22

Fergus

June

Summer holiday was meant to be relaxing. There were no classes to worry about, it was decently warm outside for Scotland's standards, and you had free time to do all the things you couldn't do during the school year. My summer was turning out to be the opposite.

With all the newly acquired free time, I'd picked up more shifts at the bookshop. When I wasn't there, I was busting my arse to get my manuscript as perfect as possible. I sent out as many query letters to literary agents and publishing companies as I could, figuring the wider I threw my net, the better chance I had of catching something.

Then there was apartment hunting. Since the proposal, Freya was at the house more often, and I'd noticed little things popping up around the home that very clearly belonged to her and not Doug or I. A gold frame on the end table with a photo from their proposal, a pastel, crocheted blanket draped across the back of the couch, and a floral apron hanging on a hook in the kitchen—just to name a few. They planned to marry before the fall semester, which meant I had just three months to find new living accommodations.

I'd scheduled a viewing of an apartment for early this morning before my shift at Graham's. Doug offered to join me, but I didn't know how much help he actually was.

"Ye cannae be serious, Fergus." His nose crinkled so much, he looked as if he were snarling at the cabinet. The door was barely hanging on, the hinges so rusted they'd surely give out before I'd even have a chance to move in.

"Och, it's no so bad."

I was lying through my teeth, and he knew it, but he just side-eyed me instead of saying anything. He didn't even bother trying to close the cabinet. Best not to damage the place before I'd even made a decision.

I picked my way into what had been deemed the living room. I'd maybe have room for my desk and a recliner, surely not a sofa. Which reminded me I'd have to purchase new living room furniture, as well as a new television. Doug had bought the one we had at home now.

He brushed his hands off against his pants as he followed me into the sole bedroom. The wallpaper was peeling, and I couldn't tell what the original color had been. Currently, it was a sickly yellow that leaned more towards brown. The window was so filthy you could hardly see out.

I didn't even want to look in the bathroom.

"At least there's no rats," I offered as a positive.

Doug wasn't impressed. "Because even the rats ken it's a shite-hole."

He was right. The place was a dump, and I'd surely catch some sort of disease, Ellen would know the name of, from all the mold. We made our way out of the flat and down the stairs to where the realtor was waiting. He plastered on a broad smile when he noticed us.

"What did we think, lads?"

I jumped in before Doug could speak. "I'm looking at a few other places and will need time to deliberate. I'll get back to ye soon."

Soon was an understatement. I'd wait a polite length of two days before I called him to turn down the flat.

We bid him farewell and escaped into the fresh air. I gasped big lungfuls of it as if that would cleanse out any mold and dust I'd inhaled. The rank smell still lingered in my nostrils, though.

Feeling a touch defeated, as this was the third less than satisfactory flat I'd visited, I turned in the direction of the bookshop, feet dragging.

"I told ye Freya and I are more than happy to have ye stay in the house. Things willna be all that different," Doug tried.

"Except the fact ye'll be a married couple and Freya will be there full time." I waved my hand dismissively. "The two of ye deserve to enjoy your marriage without me tagging along. Ye should have your privacy."

There were some things about Doug's personal life I did not need to be privy to. Specifically, what happened in the bedroom between him and Freya.

"I'll find a decent place," I assured him. "Even if I have to stray further from campus. And I'll still be working at Graham's. I can come over before or after a shift to see ye. Give Freya a break from cooking for ye all the time."

"Oi! I can cook, too," Doug scoffed.

"Maybe. But can ye cook anything edible?" I teased. "If so, I've yet to see it in all the years I've kent ye."

He roughly shoved my shoulder, causing me to stumble a few steps, and we both laughed.

It was a comfort knowing Doug was just as hesitant about the change as I was. Truthfully, he was the one going through the biggest adjustment, getting married and thinking about where he and Freya wanted to put down roots after graduation. My moving out gave us the opportunity to gradually distance ourselves, so it wasn't such a shock when we lived in different cities.

Doug's hand clamped down on my shoulder, and when I looked at him, there was a rare sadness in his eyes. As long as I'd known him, Doug had always been sunshine incarnate, brightening anybody's day with a joke or kind word.

"Ye'll always be my best mate. Ye ken that, right?

No matter where we end up."

"Ye could never get rid of me," I tried to joke, but my smile was shaky.

His smile mirrored my own. "As if I'd ever want to."

"Excuse me?!" Ellen exclaimed, causing me to hold the receiver a few inches from my ear in order to keep my eardrum intact. "They were asking how much for that cowp?"

I heaved out a sigh as I sank back, the chair groaning underneath me in sympathy. "I'll just have to broaden my search. I can drive to class or take the bus if needed."

In the end, having a decent roof over my head that wasn't filled with black mold was more important than being within walking distance of campus.

"You were kinder than ye needed to be," Ellen sniffed. "Should have told him right then and there he was off his heid for trying to lease it in such a state."

Even though it probably wasn't her intention, I found myself chuckling softly. Her irritation was funnier when it was directed at somebody else. Thankfully, that was the case more often than not since our kiss outside the dance hall.

"Now I wish ye'd been there to tell him yourself. I would have loved to see his face."

The burly man facing down petite, but feisty Ellen with fire in her eyes. She'd put the fear of God into any man, giant or not. I reached for my slice of freshly baked shortbread and bit into it as I enjoyed the mental movie playing in my head.

"What are ye eating?" Ellen questioned.

I waited until my mouth was no longer full. "I made myself a batch of self-pity shortbread," I answered.

"Self-pity shortbread?" she snorted. "I'm surprised it's not self-pity scones."

"While I love Clara's scones, shortbread is my favorite pastry. Reminds me of home," I shared. "Mam has the best recipe, and we'd come home from school to the entire house smelling of butter and sugar."

Our tea would be waiting for Euan and me, along

with slices of shortbread still warm from the oven. If I ever felt down or missed home, I'd bake a pan and eat half of it in one sitting. I could easily eat the entire thing, but Doug would give me his sad puppy eyes if I didn't leave any for him.

"And why have I never had your shortbread before?" Ellen questioned.

I pondered that for a moment as I nibbled on my current slice. "Suppose I havena been sad when you're around."

The line was quiet, and I wondered what she was thinking. It could be a number of things. I never really knew with Ellen. At least not when I said something romantic. It didn't seem as though she knew how to respond to them, which made me wonder if anyone had ever said such things to her before.

"Are ye blushing?" I asked, blunt as ever, if only to fluster her further.

She rewarded me with a loud scoff. "No."

"It's alright if ye are. I like it when ye blush and I'm a bit disappointed I'm not there to see it."

More silence before a quiet, "I'm also disappointed you're not here."

My cocky smile faltered. I missed Ellen like

crazy, but for the most part, I kept myself busy enough that the longing wasn't all I thought about. There was no avoiding it now, though. My heart felt as if it were trying to escape my chest to find her, the ache so terrible.

"Tell me about your day," I diverted the conversation. "I'm sure it was much more exciting than mine."

She indulged me, "Dr. MacTavish and I met with the research team yesterday. His colleague, Dr. Abbott, caught us up on what he'd researched previously about organ transplants. Then we discussed what his goals were for this study, specifically with the introduction of immunosuppressants. I'm eager to get started."

It was clear Ellen was in her element, and I was excited to see how the research went. She had gotten better at wording it in simple terms that made sense to me, so I could actually have a conversation with her instead of just passively listening.

"What about this weekend? Were ye able to get out and explore?" I asked hopefully.

She laughed, that question seeming to perk her up even more than talking about her job. "I cannae believe I didna tell ye the story."

I smiled and settled in for the tale, tea and a fresh slice of shortbread at the ready.

"I'm never going to a park again."

I chuckled to myself. "Why's that?"

She blew out a hard breath, the sound distorted through the phone. "I went to Hyde Park to enjoy the weather. Thought I'd read the book ye'd suggested. Which, by the way, I'm absolutely hooked."

I smiled proudly around the rim of my teacup. Before she'd left, I'd convinced her to take my copy of Charles Dickens' *Great Expectations* with her. When I'd asked if she'd ever read his works, she'd said her family read *A Christmas Carol* every Christmas Eve. While it was a great story that really tugged on the heartstrings, I liked his other publications more.

"See? I told ye. Anyways, continue." I took a bite of shortbread.

"So, I found a wee bench by the pond, away from any distractions." She scoffed, "Or so I thought. I'd barely gotten through a chapter when a bloody swan came charging towards me!"

I spat crumbs all over the dining table, and then I was flat out cackling. "What did ye do?" I managed to get out.

"I had half a mind to wallop him upside the head with the book. There was nothing left to do except make a run for it! Beast chased me a good fifty meters before finally turning back."

My laughter only got worse, the mental image of Ellen taking a book to a swan's head was more than I could handle. She gave in and started laughing as well, the most beautiful sound I'd ever heard. If only it weren't tainted by the static of the long-distance call.

"I would have loved to see ye knock out a swan with *Great Expectations*," I gasped.

Chapter 23

Ellen

"Ellen? What are you doing here so early?" Dr. MacTavish asked, breaking the complete silence I'd been encompassed in for over an hour.

I'd practically taken over one of the tables in the laboratory's conference room. Dr. Abbott, the principal investigator, had requested that everyone debrief before the consultation with a potential transplant recipient in order to give her the most accurate information possible. We'd been toiling away for weeks, and I'd tossed and turned all night, too excited to see all our hard work put to use.

I looked up from the paper I'd been furiously scribbling across and merely shrugged. "I couldna sleep."

MacTavish placed his bag on the table next to me as he claimed a seat. "Show me what you've found, then," he tipped his head towards my notes.

I rearranged things so I could slide my notebook closer to him. I highly doubted he'd be able to decipher my terrible handwriting, though.

"I've been focusing on the different immunosuppressants and their success rates thus far. I ken Dr. Abbott is more acquainted with Purinethol, but I think we should consider Azathioprine. While not as many trials have used it, the organs seem to be staying healthy longer." I tipped my head to the side. "Granted, the transplants are fairly recent, but there's still a decent amount of evidence suggesting it will continue to be successful."

Sifting through my papers, I found the data that backed up my claims. Dr. MacTavish took a closer look as I went in-depth about my ideas and reasoning for why I thought Azathioprine would be worth serious consideration.

"If we dinna take risks, then the medical field would never advance, aye?"

His moustache twitched as he smiled at me.

"Aye," he agreed. "When the other men get here, I suggest you bring this up."

My mind went blank for a moment. Typically, I kept quiet during debriefings and only shared my findings with Dr. MacTavish. I was here as his assistant, after all. I wasn't a professional like all of the others with specialist degrees and years of experience. I hadn't even completed my undergraduate yet.

"Sir..."

He stopped me with a shake of his head. "It's your research, Ellen. I willna take credit for it."

A wave of pride washed over me. "Thank ye, sir."

Now that I knew I would be presenting to the team, I returned to my proposal with renewed fervor. Dr. MacTavish assisted me as I made sure I had everything in order to share my ideas in a cohesive manner. Now was when I could really use Fergus' organizational skills. He seemed to have a knack for turning my jumbled mess into a well-thought-out plan. MacTavish's help would have to do for now.

The rest of the team joined us one by one, gathering at the other tables and conversing with each other as they enjoyed their morning coffees or teas. I was glad I didn't have to move my things to make room for them and did my best to ignore the idle chatter. Conversation halted whenever Dr. Abbott entered, and everyone else scrambled to retrieve their notes.

"Good morning. We've got just over an hour before our patient is set to arrive, and I'd like to have all our ducks in a row by then. Who'd like to start us off?" he inquired, glancing around the room.

Richard raised his hand, but it was Dr. MacTavish who spoke up. "Miss McLean has just regaled me with her latest idea, and I believe it's something we should look into further."

All eyes were on me. Dr. Abbott looked intrigued; Mr. Doyle and Mr. Nelson curious; and Mr. Richard Cross? Well, he was living up to his surname with his irritation worn blatantly on his face. However, instead of shrinking beneath their gazes, I sat up straighter, prepared to share what I'd put together.

"Miss McLean is only an assistant, MacTavish," Richard cut in. "I understand she does well in your courses, but she does not have the credentials for-"

"It's Dr. MacTavish, if you please," my professor interrupted in return. "And I have looked over her notes and see no faults in her ideas nor the data she used to inform such theories."

Richard's eyes narrowed, but he knew that even if he was above me, he was merely a research associate; a minor position in comparison to Dr. MacTavish being the partner of the principal investigator. And so his mouth stayed shut—as much as it seemed to pain him.

Nonplussed, Dr. Abbott tipped his head in my direction. "Miss McLean. Proceed."

"Thank you, Dr. Abbott." I gathered the sheets before me, even though I didn't need to look at them. "I would like to propose the idea of using Azathioprine as our immunosuppressant of choice."

When the doctor's eyebrows raised, I offered the data sheet to him. "In the long term, it has a higher success rate than Purinethol. Recipients of Purinethol report organs failing after only a few years. One transplant is risky enough for a patient, let alone several operations. Continuously weakening their immune system only increases the risk of further issues."

The room seemed to hold its breath as Dr. Abbott looked over the information, bushy eyebrows pinched together. I could feel Richard attempting to glare a hole in the side of my head, but I didn't give him an ounce of attention. I was completely focused on Dr. Abbott.

"I cannot argue with the evidence you've given me." He looked up to meet my gaze. "May I look over the rest of your notes?"

I all too eagerly handed them over to him, not even thinking to be embarrassed at the lack of legibility. The fact that he was even considering my proposal had me on cloud nine. My fingers fiddled with the fabric of my skirt under the table as he read, dark eyes scanning quickly over the pages. Dr. MacTavish sent me an encouraging smile.

Dr. Abbott finally set the papers down and directed his attention to the men on my left. "Cross, Doyle. Prepare your information for the patient." He then slid the notes over to the American statistician, Mr. Nelson. "Look over this for me, will you? Not that I doubt Miss McLean's capabilities. Rather, I doubt my own."

He sent me a knowing smile, and I felt on top of the world; Richard and his sour puss act be damned.

I'd already experienced the highlight of my day—or rather my life—so I was content to just observe during the patient consultation. We were using the medical theatre, and I thought it an odd choice of location for such a personal meeting. The room was spacious with tiered rows of seating forming a partial circle around a table and three chairs. Dr. Abbott and Dr. MacTavish took two of the seats while the rest of us made our way to the theater seating.

A secretary of the building escorted the patient in and guided her to the seat across from the doctors. We'd been given her basic information: Mrs. Gwendolyn Davies, thirty-eight years of age, and in need of a kidney transplant. Her dry skin and sickly pallor aged her considerably, and while her cheekbones were gaunt, there was swelling around her eyes that made the orbs little more than slits. Still, I could see her gaze shifting uncomfortably between the two men sitting before her and then the rest of us behind them.

"Hello, Mrs. Davies. We're glad you could meet with us today and discuss your potential transplantation," Dr. Abbott began.

I made more mental notes about the woman. Her

worn, tweed skirt was pilled where she kept fussing with the fabric, pinching and tugging at it. The near-constant jiggling of her leg drew my attention to her swollen ankles and shoes that had surely been much too big on her before her kidney began to fail her. She looked downright terrified.

Our pharmacologist, Thomas Doyle, stepped forward to debrief her on her options when it came to drugs, unintentionally towering over the poor woman.

"I-I don't understand," Mrs. Davies shook her head quickly.

Doyle repeated himself, slower, but her fidgeting only got worse to the point where she seemed to be shaking. Surely, any minute now, the metal chair beneath her would begin to rattle. Her eyes met mine, and before I could process what I was doing, I found myself standing up and approaching her.

Unlike Mr. Doyle, I knelt down in front of her, taking one of her hands away from her skirt and instead clasping it between both of mine.

"Ye have several options when it comes to which drugs we use," I murmured, my Highland lilt slipping out. But when Mrs. Davies' eyes grew a touch less panicked, I decided not to hide it. "They are meant to weaken your immune system-"

"But why would you weaken it when I'm already sick?" she quaked.

"If we dinna weaken it, your immune system will attack the donated organ. Your body will reject it." I gave her hand an encouraging squeeze. "It's only until the organ has taken root and begins to function properly. In the meantime, we will take the utmost care to provide ye with a safe environment to avoid infection or any other complications."

Mrs. Davies nodded in understanding, but the concerned lines between her eyebrows remained. "And how do I know which one to take?"

"That's what we're here for." I gestured behind me to the team. "We are working hard to understand all of the options and their viability so we can make this transplant as successful as possible. Ultimately, though, you will have the final choice of which one ye would like to take. Once ye have been presented with all the information, that is."

"I'm no good with all this...medical jargon, though."

I smiled reassuringly. "I promise we'll make it as clear as possible. But ask questions if ye dinna understand."

Her grasp on my hand was firm as she returned the smile, and it didn't weaken, even when I made to stand. Suddenly, there was the scraping of metal on wood next to me, and we both turned to find Dr. Abbott placing his chair next to Mrs. Davies. When I looked up at him, he gestured for me to have the seat.

"It would do my knees good for me to stand for a while," he explained.

I thanked him and then slid into the chair, my own knees grateful for the reprieve from squatting, and adjusted mine and Mrs. Davies' hands to be clasped more comfortably in our new position.

I practically floated the whole way home as if helium ran through my veins. When joining this study, I hadn't expected to do anything more than help Dr. MacTavish and maybe make a comment here and there. I could've never guessed I would be making suggestions to the principal investigator or interacting directly with a patient.

It killed me waiting for eight o'clock to come around so I could tell Fergus. Had it been any other night, I would've called as soon as I got home, knowing he'd be around to answer, but he had the closing shift at the bookshop tonight. I willed the hands on the kitchen clock to move faster. The moment the minute hand reached the number twelve, I dialed for the operator.

"Long-distance operator. May I help you?"

"I'd like to place a call to Edinburgh."

I shared my current number for the billing and then Fergus' name and phone number. The worst part about long-distance was the delay while the operator conducted multiple steps to connect the call. It seemed like ages until I heard the telltale ringing. I fidgeted in my seat as I waited for Fergus to answer, bobbing my foot in time with the rings until there was a click to signal that he had picked up.

"Hullo?"

"Hi!"

There was a chuckle from the other end. "Well, someone sounds very chipper. Good day, was it?"

The sound of his laugh just made me smile even wider. "Aye. Very much so."

"Alright, then. Tell me all about it."

I could hear the unreliable chair creak as he presumably settled in at his own kitchen table. My only hope was that Fergus let Doug and Freya keep the table when he moved out, or for Freya to convince Doug to buy a new one that wasn't on the verge of collapsing.

"I'm not sure what to start with," I admitted, lips pursed as I debated. "I'll start backwards. Save the best for last, aye?"

Fergus listened as I shared about Mrs. Davies, recalling how good it felt to ease her apprehension, even just a little.

"I can only imagine how grateful she was to have your kind face there. I'm quite partial to it myself," he playfully added.

Thank goodness he wasn't able to witness the deep blush in my cheeks. "I dinna think ye've ever described it as kind," I quipped, finding the taunting much more familiar.

"Well, it wasna so kind at first, but ye've softened on me," Fergus reasoned, his smug smile audible.

"Only a little," I hummed.

He chuckled softly before moving on. "Alright, ye said ye were saving the best for last."

And there it was, that feeling of immense pride again.

"Ye ken how I've been doing a lot of research on different types of immunosuppressants?"

"Aye."

"Dr. MacTavish came in while I was researching, and I shared my ideas with him. Then..." I dragged out the word, letting the tension build some. "He suggested I share them with Dr. Abbott during our team debrief."

The other end of the line was silent, but I knew it was because Fergus was just as shocked as I had been.

"And did ye?" he asked eagerly.

"Aye, and he actually seemed very receptive. Not that I think he'd really change his plans for the upcoming clinical trials, but even just being heard out is an accomplishment in itself."

"Och," Fergus scoffed. "You're brilliant. He'd be a dafty not to listen to ye."

"It's no like he has a doctorate in this exact field or anything," I replied sarcastically.

Fergus made a noise in the back of his throat that made his disagreement clear. I was grateful for his wholehearted belief in me. However blind it may be.

"That does sound like quite the day, though. I'm happy for ye, Ellen. And..." he dragged out, "I may have something to make it even better. Possibly."

"Oh? And what's that?"

Fergus seemed to find pleasure in making me wait, though I couldn't judge him too harshly, as I had just done it to him.

"A publishing agent in London reached out wanting to schedule a meeting with me."

I sat up straighter. "Fergus, that's amazing!"

"Och, it's not a contract signing. Just a meeting," he dismissed. "I'm sure they've got a dozen other authors they're consulting with. And probably ones with more experience than me."

If he were in front of me, I would have been heavily glaring at him. For as talented a writer as he was, he lacked confidence in his attractiveness to agents and publishers.

"If I can share my idea with the principal investigator and have it be taken seriously, you can get an offer from a publishing agent."

"We'll see," he brushed me off. "You're not even going to ask why it's so great for *you*?"

I shrugged. "Seeing you be successful makes me happy."

"Would actually seeing me in person make you happier?"

I nearly dropped the handset. When I'd agreed and fully committed to the study, I'd accepted that I wouldn't see Fergus for three months and our only form of communication would be through a questionable phone connection. I'd never expected him to come to London.

"Or ye don't have to. I'm sure you're busy and I dinna ken how much time Mr. Graham will be able to give me off–"

"No!" I practically shouted. "I'd absolutely love to see ye."

It was quiet on the other end before he spoke up again, his voice softer. "I'd love to see ye, too."

Chapter 24

Fergus

July

In true Fergus Morgan fashion, I had planned my trip to visit Ellen down to a T. Since she had to work, I'd taken a later train that gave me enough time to check into the hotel—which was equidistant between her flat and the research center—before meeting her for supper. While I'd taken a few minutes at the hotel to freshen up and change clothes, I'd given up on attempting to gel my curls into place and left my hair to its own devices.

It was probably all for the best as I found myself repeatedly running my fingers through the strands while I waited on a bench in the courtyard for Ellen. Any styling would have been ruined, and the curls would have had their way anyway. My body was practically buzzing knowing I'd be able to see her soon. That I'd be able to hold her, kiss her. It'd barely been over a month, but I had missed her terribly

Soon enough, people began to trickle out of the building. I kept my eyes peeled for Ellen's dark curls as the foot traffic picked up, a few women sprinkled throughout the men, but none of them were the one I was looking for.

Then I saw her.

I was frozen in place. Had she gotten even more beautiful since I'd last seen her? Was that possible? Maybe it was because her skin had gained some color, most likely from her weekends spent exploring London or reading in Hyde Park. I watched her glance around the courtyard before her eyes locked on mine, and the corner of her lips twitched into a smile.

I had the urge to run to her and scoop her up into my arms, but figured she wouldn't appreciate that, given we were just outside of her workplace. Her relaxed pace only confirmed my assumption. Once she reached me, there was no greeting of any sort.

She simply kept moving and snagged my hand as she passed.

"Come with me."

While I was confused, I didn't really have a choice. At this point, I would follow her anywhere she asked—or told—me to. I matched her stride for stride, unsure of where we were going until we reached the end of the building and Ellen pulled me around the corner.

I gasped when she pushed me up against the brick wall, "Wha–?"

But then her lips were on mine. My hands instantly found her waist, pulling her body tight to mine. It took everything in me not to groan at the feel of her. At least Ellen seemed just as eager, her restraint from only moments ago completely gone as she let go of my hand to instead cup my neck and keep me in place. Not that I had any plans to pull away from her. If we were going to stop, she'd have to be the one to initiate it. It felt as if I'd been traveling through the desert before stumbling upon an oasis, and I was going to drink my fill.

The sound of nearby laughter caused us to part, but the voices soon faded away once more. I just grinned down at Ellen, still wrapped up in my embrace.

"And here I was worried ye werena as happy to see me as I was you."

Her cheeks flushed even more. "It took everything in me to be patient enough to get you away from prying eyes."

I couldn't resist. I lowered my head to capture her lips once more and was rewarded with the softest of moans from Ellen.

"I've missed you," she practically whimpered.

My chest ached at the sound; why could I not get close enough to her? Right. Because we were in public in broad daylight. I pulled away just enough that I could press my forehead to hers, now using my grip on her waist to keep us separated in hopes of controlling my desires.

"I missed ye, too. So much," I breathed.

Her fingers gently scratched at the nape of my neck, combing through the curls there in a way that caused a chill to run down my spine. Then she took a step back to look me over. I stood up straighter under her scrutiny.

"Your curls. Ye dinna have them slicked back."

I shrugged, sheepishly running my hand through the wayward strands for about the hundredth time that afternoon. "They werena having it, so I let them win today."

She just beamed up at me. "I like it. It suits you."

Now I was the one flushing, something I only seemed to do around her. First, it'd been a flush of frustration, Ellen having a knack for getting under my skin, unlike anyone else I'd ever met. Now, she got to me in a completely different way. She'd managed to needle her way into my chest and straight to my heart.

"What do ye say to supper?" she asked, "Thought we could prepare something at my flat instead of going out."

"Sounds great," I smiled.

Much better than sitting in a busy and noisy restaurant. This way, I would have Ellen all to myself and could be as affectionate as I wanted.

Ellen beamed up at me as she slipped her hand back into mine, giving it a tug once more, and again, I followed her like the lovesick puppy I was. Even when we boarded the bus, I kept her hand in mine as we found a pair of seats together.

"How was today?" I asked, thumb stroking over her knuckles.

Ellen let out a mix between a sigh and a grumble.

"Someone must've spat in Richard's porridge this mornin', because he was being more of an arse than usual."

The woman across the aisle from us looked appalled at Ellen's choice of words, eyes practically bugging out of her head behind her spectacles, and jaw dropped wide enough she could catch flies. I had to hide my chortle with a cough. I sometimes forgot that other people weren't used to women as brazen as Ellen. While it had admittedly taken me a bit, I appreciated how confident and unapologetic she was in herself. It was one of the things I found most attractive about her. Besides those deep blue eyes of hers, that is.

I leaned in closer to her, lowering my voice. "Are ye sure ye didna finally give in to your urges and spit in his coffee?" I teased lightly.

"Oi," Ellen eyed me, but the twist of her lips told me she found the idea just as amusing. "I should have never told ye about that fantasy."

We both laughed that time.

I'd heard plenty of stories about Richard from Ellen, starting off when he'd first picked her up at the train station. He was sneaky with his demeaning comments, but his intentions were clear; he meant to make Ellen feel out of place. As if the medical world didn't do that enough. Part of me had hoped to run into the bloke while I was visiting, but I also knew Ellen wouldn't take kindly to me speaking up on her behalf. She would always want to fight her own battles. In this case, it meant letting the passive-aggressive comments slide off her back and continuing to work hard to prove her worth. And subsequently, prove him wrong.

"I cannae tell ye how many times he had me repeat myself because he supposedly couldna understand what I was saying. I wasna even letting my accent show through," Ellen huffed, slumping down a little.

I let go of her hand to instead drape my arm over the back of her seat.

"Well, I love your Highland accent," I argued, fingers dusting over her shoulder. "Even if it is crackly over the phone."

She raised a brow at me, "As a Scot yourself, I'd say you're biased. Ye also ken better what I'm saying."

I simply shrugged. I was admittedly biased about a lot of things when it came to Ellen, but I wasn't going to agree with her and give her the satisfaction.

She knew she was right, though. I could see it in the curve of her smirk before she turned her head to look out the window.

It wasn't much further until we reached the stop near her flat and made our way to the building. Ellen had described it to me when she'd first arrived, but I was still impressed by how much space she had for just one person.

"Do ye think they'd tell ye how much they pay for this?" I mused as I peeked into the restroom. "I can only imagine how much it costs if it's anything like the flats in Edinburgh."

Ellen set down her keys on the coffee table. "Still no luck?" she asked.

I shrugged, lips pressed together as I joined her in the kitchen. "I'm branching out a bit further. Figure I can stand to have a longer commute to school since it's only a year."

She began to retrieve items from the fridge, and I peered over her shoulder to see what she had.

"Haggis with neeps and tatties?"

"I've been craving it, and the haggis I've managed to find at restaurants here is so painfully bland compared to home." She opened up one of the cabinets above us. "I also got the ingredients for you to make me your famous self-pity shortbread."

Her grin was devious as she turned to me, and I chuckled. "But neither of us are feeling very pitiful, are we?"

"Let it be a celebratory shortbread, then," she amended.

Her eyes were wide and hopeful, and I had to look away, lest I be pulled into their depths.

"Alright, then. I can focus on that while ye fix supper. Fair?"

"Fair," she agreed.

The kitchen left little room for the two of us to maneuver about, but we managed without even so much as a single bump or spill. My body seemed hyper-aware of Ellen's, easily navigating around her to retrieve what I needed, whether it be a spoon or butter. She stepped aside so I could put the pan into the oven without even pausing in her preparations. I assisted with the rest of the meal while the shortbread cooked.

Soon enough, the compact flat was filled with the aroma of a traditional Scottish meal. Ellen took a deep breath in, a pleased smile on her lips.

"Smells like home," she sighed in content.

For some reason, her words caused an odd

twisting sensation in my chest. *Home.* I knew she meant her family home in Beauly. I'd experienced firsthand the delicious scents created by her mother's cooking. And it wasn't as though Ellen and I had ever cooked together in our short time of going steady. But there was a part of me that wanted her to mean Edinburgh with me. Maybe someday.

The shortbread finished first, so I carefully retrieved it and set it out to cool before cutting it into generous slices.

"Are ye gonna share any with your coworkers?"

Ellen looked at me as if I'd grown a second head. "If I did, it'd only be with Dr. Abbott and Dr. MacTavish. Most likely, though, I will be eating it all myself."

"Well, I do hope ye'd be sharing it with me, at least," I chuckled.

She gazed at me for just a moment before shrugging with a light "humph". My jaw dropped, and without thinking, I scooped her into my arms and away from the stove. Ellen let out a squeal, but then quickly clamped her mouth shut to keep in any other noises.

"What was that? Ye think ye'll get away with eating all the shortbread *I* made without giving me a piece?"

When she didn't say anything, I tickled her side which caused her to squirm even more viciously in my grasp, but I just held on tighter.

"Fine!" she gasped finally. "Ye can have a piece."

"Two." I countered.

She laughed, but nodded in assent. "Two."

"Perfect!" I gave her cheek a quick peck and then let her go.

She sent me a playful glare over her shoulder as she smoothed out her clothing and returned to the oven, but I knew she wasn't truly mad at me. I would have gotten far more than a glare if she had been.

We settled in at the table once supper was ready, my knees knocking against Ellen's underneath.

"Sorry," I chuckled, trying to adjust my long legs so we both fit comfortably.

She did the same until we finally found an arrangement that worked and didn't have me banging into the table legs either.

"So, tomorrow is my day off," Ellen began after we'd gotten a few bites down, "but you've got your meeting with the agent, right?"

I nodded while wiping the corner of my mouth with my napkin. "Aye. There are a few other agencies in London I'd thought I'd visit. Figured I might as well take advantage of being here. But ye dinna have to follow me around."

"What if I want to?" Ellen challenged lightly. "It'll be interesting to see. I ken very little about the querying process besides what ye've told me so far."

I smiled. "Alright. I'd love to have ye, then."

We ate our fill of supper and then retired to the couch to enjoy our shortbread slices. Normally, I would have had my entire slice downed within seconds, but I wanted to get Ellen's verdict on it first. She cupped her hand under her mouth to catch any crumbs as she took a bite and then looked at me with wide eyes.

"Fergus!" she managed after she'd washed it down with a drink of tea. "Now I'm really upset ye never made this for me before."

I laughed. "Well, now that I ken ye like it, I'll make it more often. I'll never say no to making shortbread."

We finished off our slices quickly after that, and Ellen went back to the kitchen to retrieve two more. On her way back, she turned on the radio, but we ended up focusing on each other more. Despite calling twice a week, we somehow still had plenty to talk about; things I forgot to tell her about Doug and Freya's wedding preparations and small tidbits from her explorations of London that had slipped her mind. All the while, we never stopped touching each other. I couldn't keep myself from playing with her fingers, marveling at how dainty they were compared to my own. And I'd lost track of how many times Ellen had reached up to push one of my curls back when it'd fall in my eyes. *Mental note: Leave hair curly around Ellen more often.*

But the clock on the opposite wall told me it was far past the appropriate hours for me to be in a single woman's flat.

"I should go."

I placed my hands on my thighs to help push myself up with a groan as my stuffed stomach protested at the sudden movement. Ellen stood much faster than I did, following me to the door and catching my hand before I could reach for the handle.

"Fergus."

I didn't have to see her expression to know she didn't want me to go; the tone of her voice said it all. Even in just the uttering of my name. I laced our fingers together as I turned, a half-hearted smile on my face, and then leaned down to place a kiss to her forehead.

"I know. Just because I *should* go, doesna mean I want to." I took a deep breath in, savoring the comforting scent of a home-cooked meal and the distinct sweet, floral fragrance that was all Ellen. "But I'm going to."

Her hand gently cupped my cheek and she tilted her head up for a soft kiss before stepping back and letting go of me completely. Then her arms crossed over her chest as she gave me a once-over.

"Why did I have to choose such a gentleman?" she tisked her tongue, shaking her head a little.

That at least made me laugh, and then she was grinning, too. I reached behind me to open the door, but kept my gaze on her, eyebrows raised. "Just remember. It was *your* choice. Ye said it yourself."

She wasn't baited. "I'm a smart lass. I ken I made the right choice."

Those words filled me up more than any hearty meal ever could, and it took everything in me not to pull her back in for a much longer goodbye kiss. But I knew I'd get lost in her and would never leave. So, I made the right choice for us now and walked out the door.

Chapter 25

Fergus

We'd visited three other agencies after my first initial meeting, and to say I was done marketing myself and my book was an understatement. Writing a book was one thing, but trying to promote and sell it was another beast entirely.

Ellen had insisted on treating ourselves to pastries and a relaxing afternoon in Hyde Park. We made sure to steer clear of any nefarious-looking swans and sought refuge under an oak near the Peter Pan statue. I leaned back against the sturdy trunk with a grateful sigh. Having Ellen next to me, arm pressed against mine, made me even happier. I'd be leaving early tomorrow morning so I could get back to Edinburgh in time for my shift at the bookshop. I'd been lucky to get the past two days off with how understaffed we were currently. I think the old man had a soft spot for me, but he'd never admit it, let alone blatantly show it.

My Chelsea bun was gone in just four bites, and I licked the glaze off of my fingers before draping my arm around Ellen to make her more comfortable. And, of course, to get even closer.

"Pastries were a genius idea," I sighed, resting my head back.

Ellen laughed softly as she nestled herself against me, still nibbling on her fruit tart. "We both deserved a treat."

"Even after all the shortbread we ate last night?" I raised a brow at her.

"Ye can never have too many treats," she reasoned.

I gasped, falling back as I clutched my chest dramatically. Treats were my love language, although I had a feeling Ellen already knew that based on prior experiences.

"See, this is why we're together."

That made her laugh as well, and I joined in, basking in the glow of her happiness and reveling in the fact that I was the cause of it. It was much more fun to make her laugh than grumble and curse at me.

We fell into a comfortable silence as we people-watched from the shade of the oak. Many were taking advantage of the warm weather, including a father and daughter who stopped at the statue for a snack break.

My fingers absently played with the ends of Ellen's hair as I let my mind wander. I thought of all I needed to do when I made it back to Edinburgh, finding a place to live being the most important. The press of Ellen's body against mine had me daydreaming about a little cottage to share with her once we'd graduated—and gotten married, of course.

Married.

Had that really crossed my mind? Maybe it was because I was constantly around Doug and Freya, and all they talked about now was their upcoming nuptials. They'd just gotten engaged in May and already had almost everything prepared for an early September wedding.

Ellen and I, however, had only been together since February and hadn't even said 'I love you' yet.

I did love her, though. I think I knew I was in love with her whenever she told me she was leaving for London, and it felt like my world had been flipped upside down. But I wasn't about to scare her off by telling her too soon. I'd let her take the lead.

The father and daughter stood, having finished their snacks, and had just started down the path when I registered a scruffy stuffed bear still sitting at the foot of the statue. I gently nudged Ellen, and she looked up at me in confusion, having been lost in her own thoughts.

"The little girl forgot her bear," I gestured towards the statue.

She sat forward so I could carefully untangle myself from her. I probably had grass or dirt on my pants, but I didn't care as I took off in a jog to the statue, snatching up the bear and turning in the direction of the father and daughter.

"Wait!" I called out, hurrying after them.

Thankfully, he turned at the sound of my voice. His expression quickly went from confusion to shock once he saw the bear in my hands, coming to an abrupt halt. His daughter followed his attention and gasped.

"Oswald!" she cried, wiggling out of her father's

grasp to run back to me.

I knelt down and held out the well-loved bear towards her. She instantly clutched him to her chest, burying her nose between the two rounded ears.

"I suppose he stayed behind in hopes Peter would take him to Neverland, but I ken he'd miss ye too much," I offered as an explanation.

Her brown eyes peeked up at me from over the toy's head, almost the same color as its fur. Then her attention was on Oswald as she held him out in front of her, her brows crinkling together adorably.

"Oswald! You're not allowed to go to Neverland without me," she scolded him. But the bear was quickly forgiven and embraced once more.

The girl's father chuckled behind her, and I stood when he offered his hand. "Thank you for catching us. I really appreciate it. Saved us both a lot of tears at bedtime."

"Of course," I brushed it off as I shook his hand.

"Do you have children of your own?"

I quickly shook my head. "Och no. I've still got a year of uni, but someday I'd like to have a few."

"Well, when you do,"—he smiled as he glanced over my shoulder at Ellen, and I blushed at the connection he made—"you'll be a great father."

All I could do was duck my head in acknowledgement of the high compliment. He thanked me again and instructed his daughter to do the same before they both waved and continued down the path. When I returned to my spot next to Ellen, I could feel her eyeing me.

"What's that blush for?"

"Nothing," I waved my hand dismissively. "The little girl was just adorable, is all."

"I saw her give the bear what looked like a stern talking-to," Ellen giggled.

I laughed as well. "Oh, I do believe Oswald will be in timeout for a while after a stunt like that."

"You're very good with children," she mused. "I remember seeing ye with the little boy at the bookshop. Ye gave him a sweet and made his entire day."

The corner of my lips curved up in a crooked smile as I thought back on the wee lad, but I just shrugged. "I was always the one having to entertain Catriona when she was a wee lassie," I reasoned.

Euan was far too immature to look after our baby sister, so the responsibility had fallen to me, and I'd absolutely loved it. I couldn't wait to have children of my own to play knights and dragons with and read bedtime stories to.

I gazed after the father and daughter wistfully. "I'm excited to have my own bairns one day," I hummed. "What about you?"

Ellen went stiff beside me. When I looked, her eyes were locked straight ahead on the water. Thinking back, I couldn't remember Ellen saying much about children or whether she wanted to have any. I knew she came from a close family, but that didn't always mean someone wanted one of their own.

She looked like she was trying to shrug, but her shoulders stayed up around her ears, almost protectively, as if she were bracing herself for this conversation. It was bound to happen, though. At some point, we'd need to discuss it if we were to continue seeing each other. My stomach knotted up.

What if-

I didn't allow myself to finish that thought. Not before Ellen had a chance to respond.

"I dinna believe I do. It doesna seem like it would be the best idea given my career choice."

My eyebrows crinkled together. "Why would that affect it? Plenty of women have careers as well as a family. I'd never expect ye to be a housewife."

I chuckled at my attempted joke, but it sounded forced. Ellen wasn't amused.

"It'll be long hours. Late nights in the labs researching or conducting clinical trials. The medical field doesna exactly lend itself well to both," she explained.

"But your mother did it," I pointed out.

"My mam *left* us," she snapped. "It was always one or the other with her. She chose to be a housewife while raising my brothers, but then she chose her career over me."

I opened my mouth to argue, but the look she gave me had me choking on my unspoken words. There was a storm in her eyes I hadn't seen in a long time.

"She left me, her only daughter, when I was just old enough to wean and didna return until I was practically ready for school. My first four years of life, and I didna have my mother because she *chose* not to be there."

I shook my head, "Ellen, ye wouldna do that. It's different for you."

"How?" she demanded. Her body was practically shaking at this point.

"There's not a bloody *war*." I did my best to rein

in my frustration, but it was difficult when she was being ignorant. "*That* was why your mam went. Because she had a calling she had to fulfill. The same one you have, except she was needed on the battlefield, and you are needed in a lab, in a hospital. You can go to work and come home to your family. She didn't have that option."

I would never diminish Ellen's experiences and I couldn't deny that having an absent mother affected a child, no matter their age. However, she had to realize her situation was different. She wasn't her mother, and, most importantly, she had the ability to make a different choice.

"I understand your job calls for long hours, but my job will be flexible. We could make our schedules align so the children are always cared for," I tried to reason.

"Well, it must be nice to have a job where ye can sit at home and work when ye want to. We cannae all have easy careers like being an author."

It felt like the time Euan had slammed me onto the ground and knocked the air out of me when we were bairns. I was stunned; no breath moving in or out of my lungs as I stared blankly at her. A part of me waited for her to apologize, but I knew I wouldn't be able to accept it if she did. At least not right now.

Instead, I stood and brushed off the seat of my pants.

"I should get back to the hotel." My voice sounded disconnected, even to my own ears. "Early train and all that."

Ellen clambered off the ground to stand. "Fergus," she tried.

I shook my head once, not even able to look at her, and she dropped it. I waited long enough for her to brush stray grass from her skirt before I started walking towards the edge of the park. Ellen silently followed, walking a few steps behind me.

I waved down a cab and wordlessly held the door open for her. She tried once to meet my eyes, but when I kept my gaze just an inch over her shoulder, she let out the softest sigh and climbed in.

We sat on the furthest edges of the back seat. I stared out the window, but I didn't register a single thing we passed. My mind was racing; multiple trains of thought barreling through and crashing into one another. The tension was so thick that the cab felt suffocating. When would I be able to breathe normally again?

I didn't turn to her until we came to a stop

outside her flat building. She paused once more with the door open, a question in her eyes as she looked back at me.

"I'll see ye when ye come back to Edinburgh," was all I managed.

I needed time—we both did—to think over our conversation. A family was a serious decision. I'd always wanted to be a father and a husband, to be more than just a provider. If Ellen decided a family was not what she wanted, the right thing to do would be to move on. Without each other. At least not in the capacity we had become accustomed to. But I didn't know if I could ever go back to acquaintances or quasi-friends. Not after having held her and kissed her. My heart would eventually override my sensible brain, and I would be making a sacrifice I wasn't sure I could live with.

Ellen pressed her lips together in a tight line, but nodded. "Goodbye, Fergus."

"Goodbye, Ellen."

Ellen

I was no better than my ex, ridiculing someone for the future they were striving for. The future they desired. After months of encouraging Fergus and raving about how talented of an author he was, I had pissed all over his career and treated it like it was a stroll in the park, despite seeing firsthand how much he put into his book. As soon as I'd said those terrible words, I regretted them. Fergus looked as if I had slapped him right across the face, and I may as well have.

Tuesday and Thursday passed without my phone ringing once. When the following Tuesday followed suit, I retired to bed early, curled up in the fetal position as if that would keep my heart from tearing out of my chest. Even though I could feel it beating steadily behind my breastbone, I wasn't entirely confident it was there. For all intents and purposes, it was back in Scotland, held by a man I hadn't expected to steal it from me.

Chapter 26

Ellen

I was sliding my notebooks into my satchel when Thomas Doyle approached me. We'd all ended up staying later than usual, so I had expected everyone to rush home as soon as we were free to go. Instead, Richard, Mr. Carmine, and Mr. Nelson were still lingering by the door, talking.

"The four of us were going to get supper and a drink at the pub down the street if ye'd like to join us," Doyle offered.

I knew they often went out for supper after clocking out, sometimes even including Dr. Abbott or Dr. MacTavish, but I had never been invited and had never bothered to ask if I could join. I couldn't deny that I felt quite pleased at having been considered this time. I didn't exactly feel up to preparing a meal this late in the evening, so the offer was more than tempting.

Maybe this meant they were beginning to accept me. We were nearly two-thirds of the way through with pre-clinical research and would be returning to our prior engagements soon enough. It was about time, honestly.

"Sure. That would be nice," I smiled politely at him. "Thank you."

He returned the smile and waited until I had my things before he walked with me to the door. The other men's conversation halted at our appearance.

"Ellen will be joining us," Doyle announced.

Richard's nose wrinkled as he looked me up and down, but he kept his mouth shut. The other two men at least smiled. I doubted I would ever be on good terms with Richard, and I was okay with that. He was the one who'd put his foot in his mouth right away and continued to do it again and again.

The four of us walked the few blocks to the pub, and Nelson quickly found us a table to sit at. I was clearly the odd one out, being the only woman, but they were also ten to twenty years my senior. It was more noticeable now that their conversations revolved around their families and not our research. Doyle told of his two young boys while Nelson spoke of grandchildren. Here I was with not even a niece or nephew to speak of.

The thought of children caused a sharp pain in my chest as I recalled my argument with Fergus. I'd thought of it often, going over all we'd said and how I could have voiced my concerns differently. Fergus didn't deserve my anger. Not when it wasn't even him I was mad at, but my mother instead. I just didn't want to repeat her mistakes and make my children feel like they weren't a priority. Who's to say how different our relationship could have been had she been present for those formative years?

My colleagues clearly cared deeply for their families and enjoyed spending time with them when they could. *But they're men*, I reminded myself. Society's expectations of a man's role in the household—and when it came to the raising of children—were vastly different than those of women. They could go home at the end of the day knowing there'd be a meal prepared by their wife and the bairns would have already been bathed.

Fergus' voice rang in my ears. *We could make*

our schedules align so the children are always cared for.

He'd meant it. Just the way he spoke about children made it clear he would be just as hands-on in their raising as my own father had been. He wouldn't be a man who went to work and came home to watch the telly while his wife took care of everything. No, his bairns would be his entire world. And his wife, too.

The idea of that wife being another woman made my empty stomach curdle.

"Here."

I looked up to find a pint of beer placed in front of me.

Doyle gave me a timid smile, "You look a bit out of sorts. This should fix you right up."

"Thank ye. Long day, aye?" I held the glass up, tipping it towards him in a cheers before taking a sip.

Doyle dipped his head towards me in acknowledgement before directing his attention back to the conversation at hand. While I was tempted to down the entire pint like I would if I'd been with my brothers or friends, I nursed the drink instead.

"So, Ellen. Who was the lad visiting you a few weeks ago?" Mr. Carmine smiled knowingly across the table at me.

Mr. Nelson looked between the two of us, utter confusion written all over his face. "A lad? Ellen had a gentleman caller?"

I rolled my eyes at the term, even though my palms were sweating at the mention of Fergus. Was he even my lad anymore?

"Saw him pick her up on Friday," Carmine grinned. "They walked off hand and hand."

At least that was all he'd seen and not me yanking Fergus around a corner to maul his face.

"He's a friend of mine from uni," I explained. "He was in town meeting with an agent about the manuscript he's querying. It's a historical fiction piece about the Great War."

"He didn't stay at your flat with you, did he?" Richard asked, looking overly scandalized.

I shook my head firmly. "He did not. He stayed at St. Ermin's Hotel. As I said, he was here on business."

Richard went to open his big mouth again, but Doyle stopped him.

"Cross. Leave the girl alone. It's none of our

business." He eyed the other two men, who at least had the decency to act sheepish.

Our food arrived then, successfully diverting everyone's attention from me. Even so, I did my best to stay out of the spotlight for the rest of the meal, only commenting here and there when I felt comfortable doing so.

With a full stomach, I just wanted to return to my flat and crawl into bed. My colleagues seemed to be of the same mindset as conversation dwindled and everyone paid their tabs.

"Are you alright getting home?" Doyle asked as we exited the pub.

Nelson and Carmine had already started walking back towards the research center. With the buses having stopped for the night, my only option was to get a cab home.

"I'm not far from here and I only had the one drink," I assured him.

He still looked hesitant, half turned away, but clearly not moving until he was absolutely sure. Richard joined us then.

"I'll wait with her until she gets a cab."

I would have never expected Richard to be the one to make such an offer. Maybe he'd had one too many drinks. That was the only logical explanation for him willingly choosing to spend more time around me, but I couldn't recall if he'd even had a pint at all.

If Doyle was as surprised as I was, he didn't show it. Instead, he bid us both a good evening before following after the other two men.

I stepped up to the curb so a passing cab would notice me. "You don't have to wait. I'll be fine."

Richard followed along beside me. "You do realize I saw that man enter the building with you. My own flat is just a few blocks away, remember?"

I looked over my shoulder at him, having to tilt my head back to see his face with how close he stood.

He just continued, "I had stopped by the market and was on my way home when I spotted you."

"He came over for dinner and then left that evening for his hotel," I repeated my statement from earlier. Then I turned back to the road, arms crossed tightly over my chest. "Not that I need to be explaining myself to you."

I didn't even notice him step closer; my attention was fixated on the road as I willed a cab to come. But then I felt his hand brush along the small of my back.

"I'm not surprised," he murmured, breath warm on my ear. "It's clear you're not a woman who follows society's rules."

I sensed him shrug, my body acutely aware of every single movement of his. When I moved away to put distance between us, he just closed it once more, hand seemingly glued to the bottom of my spine.

"No, you're a very wanton woman, indeed," he murmured huskily.

From the corner of my eye, I spotted his free hand moving to cup my face and seized his wrist, freezing his hand midair. My skin was burning with rage, my entire body an inferno.

"You are a disgusting piece of shite. I kent it the day I met ye and ye've proved it every day since." I practically threw his hand away from me. The motion at least caused his other hand to finally detach from my back. "Do not *ever* touch me again!"

A cab turned the corner and I waved it down frantically. I was willing to step out into traffic at this point if it meant I'd get away from Richard. Or better yet, that a car would take him out for me. The cab hadn't even pulled to a stop before I reached for the handle, jumping in and slamming the door shut behind me.

"Are you alright, ma'am?" the driver asked urgently, his eyes bouncing from me to Richard, still on the curb.

"Just drive, please."

I don't think I'd ever been in a cab that took off so fast.

Even as Richard disappeared behind us, my body continued to shake with adrenaline. While I would never be a woman who needed the assistance of a man to fight her battles, there was nothing I wanted more in that moment than Fergus beside me to comfort and assure me.

When the morning came, I still couldn't shake the feeling of Richard's hand on my lower back. The idea of facing him at work only made the queasiness worse, but there was no way in hell I was going to allow that man to think he had any sort of power over me.

I arrived early, but instead of going to the

conference room, I made my way straight to the office Dr. MacTavish shared with Dr. Abbott. The door was open, and I was relieved to find Dr. MacTavish behind one of the desks. He looked up at my entrance and started to smile, but it dropped the instant he took me in.

"Ellen. Are you alright?"

"I need to speak with you," the words rushed out of me.

He gestured to one of the seats in front of him, and I hurried to take it, tucking my hands under my legs lest they fiddle nervously in my lap.

"Let me close the door," he said, already standing.

My body relaxed at the sound of the door softly clicking shut. I felt safe with Dr. MacTavish. Out of everyone here, he was the one I trusted most.

He didn't push me to talk. He just sat down in his seat and waited patiently. I'd rehearsed what I would say a thousand times over on the way here, but as always, I struggled with organizing my thoughts into a cohesive sentence.

"We-" I started, but then shook my head. *Give the facts, Ellen.* "Last night, I joined the team for supper at the pub down the road. I thought it would be good to spend time with them outside of the study."

Dr. MacTavish bobbed his head once in understanding. I took a deep breath, but my nails still dug into the leather seat beneath me.

"When it was time to leave, Richard-I mean, Mr. Cross offered to stay behind and make sure I got into a cab safely. I was fine on my own, but he insisted, and not wanting to make a fuss, I allowed it. Mr. Cross, however..." I swallowed thickly.

The tickling sensation at the base of my spine returned, and I squirmed as if I could escape it. I couldn't even meet MacTavish's eyes, my gaze locked on the fountain pen he'd been using when I'd entered.

"He invaded my personal space and said things..."

Dr. MacTavish held up a hand, and I stopped, pressing my lips together to keep them from quivering. Why was I tearing up over this now?

"You don't have to finish. You've said and been through enough. I won't have you repeat it." He sat up straighter in his chair, his lips pressed in a firm line beneath his snowy moustache. "I'll talk with Dr. Abbott, and we will handle this. Those behaviors are never acceptable, whether on the job or not. Mr. Cross will be removed from the study immediately. It is your choice if you would like to work today or if you would prefer to go home. I think a day off is more than warranted."

The idea of sitting in my flat alone was somehow even less appealing than going and facing the rest of the team.

"I'd like to continue my work today, if ye dinna mind."

He gave me a gentle smile. "Very well. Abbott will be here any minute, and I will speak with him."

I finally met his gaze straight on. "Thank you, sir. For everything. All of the support you've given me."

"I couldn't have asked for a better assistant."

I dismissed myself then and made my way to the lounge in search of tea to calm my nerves. The chamomile tea bags had been restocked, and I thanked whatever higher power was smiling down on me and giving me this little piece of grace.

Once it was ready, I took my steaming mug over to the seat by the window. It was a gloomy day, but the view from this floor of the building was still beautiful. I took a sip, and my entire body melted as the warm liquid coursed through my system. It was the most relaxed I'd felt in nearly twelve hours.

Dr. MacTavish would handle it. I'd done what I needed to. Richard was the one who had put his job at risk.

I nursed my tea and watched a small flock of magpies foraging in the courtyard until I needed to report to the conference room. The sound of stern voices grew louder the closer I got. Upon opening the door, I found a red-faced Richard throwing his things into his bag. His head snapped up at the sound of the door, and I froze under his fiery gaze.

"Are you happy?" he snarled. "You finally got rid of me."

Dr. Abbott gripped his arm, but Richard yanked it away, momentarily turning his glare onto the elderly man before it returned to me. Now he was laughing, a cruel laugh, as he hooked his bag onto his shoulder.

"You do realize the only reason you're here is for an equity grant, don't you? Why else would they allow a *woman* into a medical research study? They needed the money. That's all. It's not as if they were actually going to let this be a career for you."

"That's enough!" Abbott barked, grasping his arm once more, but much firmer this time.

Surprisingly strong for a man pushing his mid-seventies, he began to drag Richard towards the door. I quickly darted out of the way, not wanting to be anywhere near him.

The door slammed shut behind them, and it felt as if the air had been sucked out of the room, the space unnaturally silent despite being occupied by five people. I could feel Mr. Nelson, Doyle, and Carmine staring at me. I held my head high and made my way to my usual spot at the table.

"He was wrong. I hope you know that."

I looked up to find Mr. Carmine looking at me with concern.

Doyle scoffed next to him. "And a liar. Where on earth did he come up with this equity grant idea? I *wish* we had received a grant."

That caused a few chuckles, and even I cracked a grin.

"I'm glad he's gone. They got rid of the weakest link." Mr. Nelson sent me an encouraging smile. "He's an idiot if he thought it was you."

I opened my mouth to thank them all, but then the door opened once again, and we all turned to find Dr. Abbott standing there, his face a little flushed.

"Miss McLean. May I speak to you in my office?"

he requested.

And there it was. The tell-tale dropping out of my stomach when I was called into the office of a superior. I reminded myself I had no reason to be in trouble. He probably just wanted to talk to me for HR purposes.

I followed him back into the office and once again took a seat in a leather armchair, this time in front of Dr. Abbott's desk.

"First things first, I wanted to thank you for coming forward about Mr. Cross. I'm sure it wasn't easy, and I appreciate your bravery."

All I could do was nod, ready to put this all behind me. Richard was gone, and I'd never have to deal with him again. Done and done.

"However, there is something far more important I wanted to speak to you about." He adjusted in his seat and rested his forearms on his desk, hands clasped together. "We will be conducting the preclinical trials in Edinburgh next year, and I would like to have you on my team. It's my understanding you will have your degree by then, am I correct?"

I was gobsmacked. All knowledge of the English language completely left my mind, and I probably looked like a damn herring just gaping at Dr. Abbott. I managed to pull myself together long enough to get out a 'yes, sir'.

"I think you will be a wonderful asset, Miss McLean. What I've seen of you during this study has been impressive, to say the least. You're exceptional when it comes to the research, but your interaction with Mrs. Davies is what really sold me. You're not only a brain. You have a big heart as well and to be successful in the medical field, you must have both."

Comforting Mrs. Davies had been nothing more than me wanting to make a fellow woman feel less intimidated. I didn't do it for attention or any other reason. It was all for her. I'd leaned into my natural, feminine tendency to nurture, and that softness had been seen by medical professionals as a strength, not a weakness.

"I completely agree, sir, and I can't tell you how honored I would be to join your team," I gushed.

He rearranged some papers on his desk, bringing a particularly fresh sheet to the forefront. He glanced over it before sliding it across his desk towards me.

"This is the contract. You will be paid a salary. The exact amount is listed in paragraph three." He lightly tapped the page with his pen. "I hope you find it agreeable."

My eyes didn't even register the numbers. Just the fact that I would be *paid* was agreeable enough for me. I would be a paid staff member of a clinical trial that would significantly change the medical world as we knew it. What more could I want?

Chapter 27

Fergus

"So, what's going on with you and Ellen? Are ye still together?"

I rolled my eyes at the intrusion. "Why yes, Doug. Of course, ye can come in."

I turned in my chair to level him with a look, letting him know just how unimpressed I was by his timing and his topic. I'd been in the midst of looking over the feedback the agent in London had sent me and noting which adjustments I needed to make to my manuscript in order to move forward.

Completely ignorant to my sarcasm, Doug plopped down onto the end of my bed. "Have ye talked to her since your visit?"

"She hasn't called," I shrugged.

And neither had I, but I was the one who had been belittled. Not her. I had been trying to reassure her of her capability to be both a successful scientist and mother, and she had made me feel less than because of my choice of career.

But I knew Ellen, which meant I knew she didn't truly mean what she had said. She felt backed into a corner, and her instinct was always to lash out in those situations. That knowledge didn't exactly make her comment hurt any less. Worse, though, was the realization that our plans for our futures didn't align.

"What happened in London?" Doug asked gently, a concerned crease between his brows.

I looked down at my lap, pressing my palms against each other. "Ellen doesna want children. She doesna think she can be a good mother while still having a career."

His brows only crinkled further. "Why would she think that?"

"Her mam left for the war when Ellen was just a wean and her Da raised the four of them alone until the war ended. I explained that her situation was different from her mam's, but she wasna being reasonable."

The absence of her mother had clearly affected Ellen more than either of them probably realized. While she had a perfect example of how a man and woman could go against gender norms and share the responsibilities of child-rearing, it hadn't exactly been fifty-fifty in those first few years.

"I dinna want to give up on the future I've planned," I breathed out, my voice slightly shaky at the possibility.

My life was already changing so much with my living situation being vastly different from what I'd become accustomed to in the last three years, graduation looming, and my career as an author currently in the hands of someone else. Completely altering the life I'd been striving for would be too much for me to handle.

"Ye've always spoken of having an entire gaggle of bairns. Even when we were just weans ourselves," Doug recalled.

I chuckled, "I may have been a bit of an old soul back then."

"That's an understatement," he scoffed.

"Hey." I nudged his leg. "Someone had to be the responsible one between us, and it definitely wasna going to be you."

He raised his hands defensively and tilted his head to the side. "I cannae argue that."

Our chuckles died off, and the somber cloud crept back over us. I sucked in a deep breath and held it for a moment before letting it out.

"I want bairns, but I want Ellen, too."

The last few weeks of not speaking to her had been absolute torture. When I'd received feedback from the agent, she was the one I'd wanted to call first. I wanted to tell her about the flat I'd found and how close it was to Masson Hall.

"There's still a chance ye can have both," Doug assured me. "I'm sure she's thinking about it just as much as you are. The two of ye will work it out."

"I hope so."

He clapped me on the shoulder, making sure I truly looked at him this time. "She's crazy about ye, Fergus. Anyone can see how head over heels ye are for each other."

"Thank you, Doug," I responded sincerely.

I couldn't have chosen anyone better to be my best mate. Doug had a knack for talking me off the ledge when my thoughts began to spiral. He'd sure done it enough times in the years we'd been friends.

The phone rang, and Doug let out a sigh before pushing himself up from the bed. "I'll get it."

I attempted to return my attention to my manuscript, but couldn't focus.

"Fergus! It's for you!" he called out.

I pushed my chair completely back and made my way to the kitchen. The only calls I seemed to get anymore were from my mam pestering me about my search for a flat. She'd tried a handful of times to convince me to just move back home and commute. As if driving over an hour to school was nothing.

I took the handset from Doug and placed it to my ear. "Hullo?"

The other line was quiet for a couple of beats before the person said my name, voice soft and unsure. My heart stopped for a moment. Ellen.

"I-I'm sorry if I'm no supposed to call ye, but I had exciting news and—" I heard her take a deep breath. "And you were the first person I wanted to tell."

My heart did a flip in my chest. God, it felt good to hear her voice.

"Of course I want to hear your good news," I assured her, leaning against the wall.

She didn't hesitate a second longer. "Dr. Abbott

invited me to join his team for the preclinical trials next year."

I was going to be sick. She'd be back for the school year and then she'd be off to London again. My mind began scrambling to find ways to make it work. We'd have both graduated by then. Should I need to, I could move to London, but it really hadn't been my top choice of city to live in, and I'd have to rethink my five-year plan. Again.

"T-that's wonderful," I stammered, trying my best to sound supportive.

It sounded as if Ellen were giggling on the other end, but the sound was muffled. Surely, I had been mistaken.

"Ye wanna ken the best part?" She didn't even wait for me to respond, not that I thought I was capable of anything more than a hum at this point. "The clinical trials are in Edinburgh."

The handset slipped out of my grasp, clattering against the wall when the cord caught it before it could hit the floor. I scrambled to snatch it back up and then clutched the receiver to my ear so hard it pinched.

"Wait. So ye mean ye'll get to do it here? In Edinburgh? A full-blown clinical trial with patients and everything?"

Now she was definitely laughing. "Yes! Oh, Fergus, I about died when he offered it to me. I'll have a salary and everything! I've read over the contract five times now and I still cannae believe it's real."

"Of course, it's real, Ellen. I tell ye all the time how bloody talented ye are."

"You do," her voice softened. "Suppose I should listen to ye more often."

"Can I get that in writing? No one will believe Ellen McLean just said that to me."

"Oi, come off!" she laughed, and I just soaked it up.

I didn't know it was possible to miss someone this much. There was nothing I wanted more than to have her here so I could hug her and properly celebrate. The discussion about our future could wait if it meant I got to enjoy her utter euphoria for a little while longer. But then the line grew quiet, and I could feel the shift in her mood even with all the miles between us.

"There's something else I wanted to tell ye. I almost called last night, but I needed some time to process it first."

Having a feeling it wouldn't be good news, I sat down in the kitchen chair closest to me.

"What is it?" I asked softly.

"I joined the team for dinner last night and Richard crossed a line," she began. "He started talking about how he'd seen you come to my flat and made suggestions we'd…"

I could finish that sentence for her even though I didn't want to. "That's none of his business."

She laughed, but there was no humor in it. "Exactly what I told him. And Mr. Doyle, too. But later, when he was waiting with me for a cab, he brought it up again. Only this time was different. He touched me and began talking about how he wasna surprised I had loose morals."

My blood ran cold as ice, but I could feel a flush racing up the back of my neck to my face. It was a miracle the handset didn't crack within my grip. "What do ye mean he touched ye, Ellen?"

"Placed his hand on my back. He tried to touch my face, but I caught his arm before he could and shoved it away."

A long string of curses and expletives escaped me. All the things I wished I could say to that sorry excuse for a man. What I really wanted was to put my hands on him, see how he liked being touched.

"I reported him," Ellen was quick to add. "Dr. Abbott fired him right away."

While it wasn't the most satisfying, at least it was something with lasting consequences for him. Surely being fired for sexual harassment would be recorded somewhere for all future prospective employers to see. He'd be lucky if he ever worked in the medical field again.

"Are ye alright?"

"Yes, I'm alright," she promised.

The line was quiet, and I could hear the ever-present crackle from the long-distance connection, reminding me how far away she was. I needed her near so I could reassure myself she was, in fact, fine.

"Only a few more weeks and then I'll be home." It was as if she could read my mind. "We can have that talk. I-if you're still interested."

I nodded even if she couldn't see me. "Of course I am. I'm ready for ye to be home."

Home. With me.

"Me, too."

Chapter 28

Ellen

August

My stomach was in knots knowing I'd finally be back in Edinburgh again—back with Fergus. The jostling of the train didn't help my queasiness. I was not a fan of this new trend my body had of being absolutely sick with nerves, especially when I had to spend hours in a confined space.

The elderly woman next to me leaned across the aisle, wrinkled hand extended. "Here, dearie. Try a ginger chew. It'll help settle your stomach," she encouraged.

I took the small wrapper from her. Just the idea

of consuming anything had my stomach turning, but I knew the benefits of the ginger would be worth it in the long run.

"Thank ye," I smiled gratefully.

She sent me a soft smile and then sat back in her seat, hands settling over her carpet bag as she returned her attention to the window. I did the same as well, trying to focus on the Scottish hills in the distance and not the chew as I popped it into my mouth. We would be nearing Edinburgh any minute, the landscape growing more recognizable the closer we traveled. My fingers fiddled with the empty wrapper in my hand.

While Fergus and I had not returned to our routine of calling twice a week, we'd at least spoken a handful of times in my last weeks of living in London. He'd officially moved into his new flat. More excitingly, he'd signed a contract with the publishing agent in London and had sent off his final manuscript for the agent to begin proposing. I promised him we'd properly celebrate both of our accomplishments when I returned. Celebratory shortbread included.

But first, we needed to discuss the argument. More so, the content of it and where the two of us now stood.

The train whistle was deafening as we pulled into the station and what little I could see of the platform from the opposite side of the train car was covered in a cloud of steam, the travelers milling about merely dark shadows. I stood to retrieve my luggage from the overhead compartment.

"I take it the ginger helped then, aye?" the old lady grinned.

I smiled appreciatively. "Aye, it did. Thank ye, again."

I exited the cart first and then set my suitcases aside to assist her down the steps. Once she was settled on the platform, I loosened my hold of her hand only for her to grip on tighter, leaving me no choice but to meet her dark eyes, warm like a fresh cup of coffee.

"Whatever it is that has ye worried so, ken it'll pan out the way it's supposed to. What's meant for ye will no go by ye, my mother always said."

With that, she simply gave my hand a pat, retrieved her large bag, and toddled off into the crowd. I stared after her retreating form until the jostle of a strong shoulder into mine snapped me back into reality, and I hurried to pick up my luggage. I dodged around people the best I could, but I made little progress at actually getting out of the mass of humans.

"Ellen!"

My steps hesitated, unsure amongst all the commotion if someone truly had called out my name. Ellen was quite a common name, though, so I continued along my path, ducking around two gentlemen who had no intentions of moving.

"Ellen McLean!"

I came to a complete stop and turned in a circle, searching for the source of the call. Just then, Fergus' head popped up over the shoulder of one of the gentlemen I'd just passed, sapphire eyes locked on mine. My suitcases clattered to the ground once more as I took off running, shoving my way through the crowd without any consideration for others until I collided with him.

I wasn't sure which one of us was holding the other tighter. There was a chance I'd suffocate in the fabric of his shirt, but I couldn't imagine a better way to go than engulfed in the scent of coffee and old books while held securely in his embrace.

When we finally pulled away, Fergus instantly cupped my face in his hands and leaned down towards me. I lifted on my toes to meet him halfway for the kiss, my own hands holding tight to his wrists.

"I love you." The words rushed out of me like a river flowing into the ocean. There was no stopping them. I didn't regret them, though. Not even when Fergus leaned back to look at me, eyes wide.

"You what?" The corner of his lips twitched as he scanned my face.

I giggled softly before lifting my chin, my chest swelling with confidence. "I love you," I repeated, slower this time.

He lifted me suddenly, and I let out a squeal, but Fergus quickly muffled it by covering my lips with his once more. I buried one of my hands in his loose curls as I returned the kiss. He hadn't slicked them back today.

He set me down on my feet, but didn't let go, his forehead still pressed to mine.

"Say it again?" he requested, voice soft and breathy.

My head fell back with a laugh, and he just grinned at me, a mischievous sparkle in his eyes I hadn't realized I'd missed so much.

"I love you, Fergus."

He was absolutely beaming now. "I love you, too, Ellen."

I felt as though my heart would burst right out of my chest, my ribs no longer strong enough to contain it.

Fergus' new flat was roughly the size of the one I'd had in London, though the kitchen was somehow even more compact. Freya had encouraged him to take the sofa, using it as an excuse to get a new one. I'd never thought I'd say I was happy to see a sofa, but I let out the most ridiculous sigh when I sank into the well-worn cushions.

Fergus chuckled as he took the seat beside me and like a magnet, I found myself moving closer to him until my leg pressed against his.

"I've spent a lot of time thinking about what ye said." There was no sense beating around the bush. It was best to just get straight to it. My hand found his, and I interlaced our fingers. "You were right. I'm not my mam and this isna the world we were living in when she made her choice."

So much about my situation compared to my mother's would be different. Even if there was a war, I wasn't a nurse. I wouldn't be caring for patients on the front lines. I was a behind-the-scenes person, researching and improving the medical field so those nurses could do their jobs to the best of their abilities. There would be no choosing between my purpose and my family.

"And what about children?" he wondered, the nerves clear in his voice.

Something stirred in my chest, a mix between excitement and anxiety, but I supposed everyone felt that way when it came to the prospect of parenthood. Being responsible for the care of little humans and building the foundation for their futures was intimidating, to say the least.

"I've honestly never allowed myself to even consider it. I'd been convinced it was one or the other, so I found it best to save myself the heartache and not think about it."

I looked up into those blue eyes I loved so much. I could just imagine a little, curly-haired boy with eyes just like Fergus'.

"But I've realized I'd *love* to have bairns of my

own," I confessed. "Wee ones to take on nature walks or strolls along the shore collecting shells. Teach them about the beauty of the Earth and all we can learn from it."

The more I'd thought about it, the more I'd fallen in love with the idea of being a mother. While mine had made choices I didn't agree with, I could still say she was the best mam I could have asked for. Sure, I wouldn't be perfect, but no parent was.

"Sounds like ye'll be the favorite," he teased lightly, thumb stroking over my knuckles.

"I'm sorry for suggesting that being an author was a less important job." I shook my head, "I dinna ken why I said that to ye when I've seen how hard you've worked on your novel. I mean, you traveled to bloody Beauly for an interview!"

Fergus tried to shrug it off. "I backed ye in a corner."

"That's no excuse," I argued lightly, not about to have him let me off easy. "I was wrong for it and I'm sorry."

"I forgive ye," he assured me, pressing a kiss to the back of my hand.

My chest felt lighter now, and I moved to nestle into his side, resting my head on his shoulder. He wrapped his arm around me and pressed his lips to my temple. I could feel his heart beating, strong and steady in his chest, and my own heart rate slowed to match his. Fergus; always the calm to my chaos.

"Soooo...about that celebratory shortbread..." I tipped my head back to raise my eyebrows at him and grinned.

"Oh, I've already made each of us our own batch."

Chapter 29

Fergus

September

I never thought I would prefer to wear a kilt rather than a full suit for Doug's wedding, but here I was, dreaming of the breeze a kilt would grant me. We weren't even outside yet, and I was melting. The room we'd been assigned for pre-wedding preparations had no air flow at all. Doug and I had barely managed to crack open the singular window a measly inch or two after nearly half an hour of fighting it. I'd decided to leave my dress shirt unbuttoned, determined not to be fully dressed until absolutely necessary.

For once, I was the calm one, and Doug was the flurry of nerves. He'd practically worn a path into the hardwood with his pacing. I sprawled out on a chair, trying to keep my limbs as far away from my overheated body as possible.

"Doug. You're going to make yourself sweat even more than ye already are. We dinna have a spare shirt for ye."

He stopped in his tracks and gave me a sheepish look before retiring to the other chair. "I just want it to hurry up and be here. This waiting game is killing me."

"Should've eloped," I teased.

He narrowed his eyes at me. "Ye ken well Freya would never go for it, and neither would her parents. They've made such a big deal about getting all the family here for the ceremony."

And it was a big family at that. However, Doug and Freya had at least decided to keep the bridal party minimal, with me serving as best man and Ellen as Freya's maid of honor. I hadn't seen Ellen since we'd parted ways this morning, but I couldn't wait to see her dressed up.

"Just a little longer and then ye'll be with your bride. I'm sure she's just as anxious as you are."

I didn't miss the loving smile that overtook Doug's face until a knock at the door caused us both to jump. As the best man, I'd taken it as one of my duties to answer the door and deal with whoever was on the other side. The priest had already stopped by a handful of times to talk with Doug.

However, when I opened the door, it was definitely not the priest who'd come knocking. Instead, I was met with the loch blue eyes of my girl. That is, until they wandered lower. In my hurry, I hadn't bothered to fix my shirt, and it still hung wide open.

Ellen had never seen me in anything less than a short-sleeve button-up or polo shirt. She definitely hadn't ever seen my bare torso. While I felt heat creep up the back of my neck, I didn't move to cover myself.

It seemed to take Ellen a moment to register that she was staring—and not at my face. I smirked down at her, letting her know I'd noticed her distraction, but then she thrusted a paper towards me.

"Freya asked me to give this to Doug," she explained, her words rushed.

I took the parchment from her, recognizing Freya's loopy handwriting.

"Doug wrote a letter for her, too." I took a step back into the room. "Just a second."

The neatly folded paper was lying on a nearby table. I passed it to Ellen, and she eyed the letter before raising a brow at me, her hip popping out adorably. Okay, actually it was very sexy. This whole standing around her practically shirtless was really messing with my head.

"How much of this did you write?"

"Hey!" Doug called out behind me. "I am more than capable of writing my own love letter, thank you very much."

Ellen just grinned, and I shook my head at her mischievousness. Then I leaned down to whisper in her ear and was rewarded with the softest gasp when my lips brushed her ear.

"I definitely gave him some pointers," I shared before standing straight once more.

She giggled, but quickly muffled it with her hand before pretending to seal her lips and lock them. I took the opportunity to look her over. She was all dolled up and ready for the ceremony, baby's breath pinned in her loose, dark waves. A stray lock of hair had fallen in her face, and I couldn't resist reaching up to brush it back behind her ear.

"Ye look stunning, Ellen."

She blushed adorably, her cheeks a bright rosy pink as she ducked her head. "Thank ye."

I would have leaned in for a kiss, but then Doug stomped over to us. "Can the two of ye stop flirting and give me my damn letter?"

I had the strong urge to shove him away, but I knew I would be the exact same way had I been in his shoes, and there was a letter from Ellen waiting for me. So, I handed over Freya's note, and he hurried away to read it in privacy.

"I'd better get this back to Freya so we have enough time to fix her makeup before the ceremony. This will surely have her in tears."

She made to turn, but I reached out and grabbed her wrist, gently pulling her back to me as I leaned down to steal a kiss. Ellen made a small noise of surprise against my lips, but then she kissed me back.

"Make sure they fix your lipstick, too," I winked at her before ducking back into the room and closing the door behind me.

I'd assumed that at my childhood best mate's wedding, my attention would be completely on him and his bride as they promised each other forever, but that was an extremely difficult thing to do when I had Ellen standing across from me. She was an absolute vision in a dark emerald bridesmaid dress; the antithesis to Freya in front of her, covered in white lace with her blonde waves pinned up intricately beneath the veil. Surely, Doug wasn't paying any more attention than I was to the priest's droning.

Ellen's gaze met mine once more, and I smiled crookedly. That is, until she rolled her eyes and then subtly tilted her head towards the officiant.

"Ahem," he cleared his throat, looking at me pointedly. "The rings?"

"Oh!"

All of the guests chuckled as I sheepishly retrieved the rings from my inner pocket and placed them in the priest's expectant hand. I at least managed to stay focused on the soon-to-be newlyweds as they recited their vows and were pronounced husband and wife, applauding and cheering with the rest of the guests. Doug, ever one for the dramatics, dipped Freya as they shared their first kiss as husband and wife. Freya ate it up.

They started down the aisle, and I waited until they had reached the end before offering my arm to Ellen so we could follow behind them.

"You are a mess," she whispered out of the side of her mouth.

I shrugged. "What can I say? I was distracted by a beautiful lass."

She rolled her eyes, but I saw the embarrassed smile on her lips.

The next hour was filled with photographs and mingling. Ellen and I got separated whenever Doug's parents pulled me over for a chat, and she wandered elsewhere. Then it was one relative after another grabbing me to catch up, most of them having known me since I was a wee bairn running wild with Doug. I lost track of how many times I was heckled for the ring blunder and how many drinks had been nudged my way.

But then Doug and Freya entered the room, and the celebration truly began, a live band taking the stage to start the dancing. I spotted Ellen sitting at a table by herself and sidled up beside her, pretending to casually sip at my drink as I watched the crowd on the dance floor.

"There's a lass I've been eyeing all evening. I'd like to ask her to join me for a dance, but the last time I asked, she told me she couldna dance," I sighed helplessly.

I could see Ellen turn to me in my peripheral vision. "If I recall, I gave in to your nagging and ended up dancing with ye."

I held back a laugh as I stepped closer to set my glass down next to hers on the table, having to lean down to do so and subsequently making myself eye level with her. Her expression was smug, and amusement danced in her eyes.

"Nagging, eh? Is that what I need to do now?"

She took a beat to respond, but then she shook her head. "No. I'll say yes the first time ye ask."

My brows rose in surprise and a hint of suspicion. "Every time I ask?"

"Every time," she promised.

I grinned as I stood straight, eagerly holding out my hand for her. She allowed me to guide her onto the dance floor, and I made sure we kept to the less populated edges. Ellen still had two left feet after all. But I'd happily dance with her every chance I got.

We stumbled our way through a handful of upbeat songs, Ellen tripping over the hem of her dress and bumping us into someone on several occasions. I was always there to catch her, though, scooping her into the safety of my arms.

I kept her there when the band transitioned into a slow song, moving to rest my hands on her waist as she draped her arms around my neck. The crowd thinned out as some people left the dance floor. Doug and Freya continued to slow dance in the center, and it was easy to see that for them, they were the only two people who existed in that moment. Doug looked at Freya with so much love, it felt almost intrusive to witness such blatant adoration.

"That's going to be us soon," I nodded towards them.

Ellen looked over her shoulder and smiled at the sight, but then her brows furrowed in confusion when she turned back to me. "Soon?"

My confidence didn't falter as I subtly pulled her closer so her body pressed against mine, and our faces were mere inches apart.

"Aye. Soon," I promised.

It started with just the corner of her lips tugging up, but then the dazzling smile of hers I adored so much stretched across her face.

"Okay," she breathed out.

I pressed my forehead firmly to hers. "Okay."

I kissed her then, a kiss that promised many more for years to come. Ellen was mine, and I was hers. Forever.

Epilogue

Fergus

September 2025

I pulled the small, leather box from the trunk full of Ellen's belongings and used my thumb to nudge the lid open. Nestled on a velvet pillow was a gold band with a sapphire perched on top, held in place by trefoil knots on either side. I could still picture it on her hand; when I'd officially proposed and first slipped it on her finger, when I'd promised her forever in front of all our loved ones, and when I'd sat at her bedside and held her hand in her final moments.

The image of the ring turned watery, and I

quickly blinked away the traitorous tears before turning to face Alec, holding out the box to him.

He gazed reverently at the ring. "I remember her sitting in the garden telling me about sapphires. The chemical makeup of them and the minerals that needed to be present to give it a blue hue. Half of what she said went over my head, but I was content to listen to her Highland lilt no matter what she was saying."

"Aye, I ken the feeling well," I chuckled softly. After all, I'd spent almost sixty years doing just that.

Drawing my mind back to the present, I lightly tapped a finger against the side of the box. "It'll look bonnie on Lydia, and your Grannie would be happy for her to have it. She'd be proud of ye."

Alec's eyes met my own, and I could see the emotions swimming in their dark brown depths. While the color was nothing like Ellen's deep blue, I had always been able to tell exactly what Ellen and Alec were feeling just by looking in their eyes.

"I can't say thank ye enough, Grandad. I ken how special this is to ye and-"

I waved him off before he could continue. "It's exactly where it needs to be. I ken it in my bones. This ring was made for your Lydia just as much as it was made for my Ellen. Us Morgan men are truly lucky."

He wrapped me in a firm hug then, and I held him just as tightly, unsure of who was comforting whom. What I did know was that even when my memories of Ellen were completely gone, that ring would carry on our story. And boy was it a damn good story.

Acknowledgements

I have so many more people to thank this time around, which is not a bad thing at all! (Especially as someone who often struggles to ask others for help.)

First off, thank you to everyone who read *Falling for Scotland* and took a chance on me as an indie author. I could never have imagined that I would be a self-published author. Even when I decided to publish my first novel, I didn't plan on it becoming such a big part of my life, but I have loved every minute. I've made so many friends on this journey and have grown so much as both an author and just as a person. I'm excited to see where this path continues to take me!

Thank YOU, reader, for picking up this novel, whether you've read *Falling for Scotland* or not. I appreciate your support, and I hope you loved these characters as much as I do.

Clover Callahan, thank you for helping take this story from an angsty, pre-teen draft to a full-blown, adult novel. You listened to all my chaotic thoughts and ideas and helped me polish them down into a beautiful story that I am so unbelievably proud of. (Does that make you the Fergus to my Ellen?). I can't thank you enough for your feedback, guidance, and, most importantly, your friendship. Finding a kindred spirit in you has been one of the biggest highlights of this author venture.

To my beta readers, Christen and Leslie, thank you for the confidence boost when I was deep in the depths of imposter syndrome. You hyping up this story gave me the push I needed. I'm so glad the KC book community brought me to both of you, and I can't wait for all the adventures we have ahead of us. Hockey season cannot come soon enough!

Lori, I am always so grateful to have you as my writing buddy. Thank you for always being there when I've stared at a word or sentence so long it no longer makes sense, for loving my characters as if they were your own, and for all the support you give me. It has been a pleasure getting to assist you in publishing your own debut novel. Middle school Kaitlin and Lori would be losing their minds knowing that we are legit authors. We made them proud!

If you are a reader and you've made it this far,

make sure you check out *Choosing Chopsticks* by Lori Scoby. Just saying.

Thank you to my editor, and fellow KC local author, M. A. Kilpatrick for finding all the missing commas and words that had magically disappeared during edits.

Thank you, Jane from Torch Lit Ink PR, and all the ARC readers for the love you've shown *Falling for Ellen*. Jane, you have been so great to work with. You took a process I found intimidating and made it easy and fun! Thank you for helping me bring Ellen and Fergus out into the world.

To all the indie bookstores that I've worked with, you are amazing! It's so inspiring to see you all living out your dreams and helping nurture this wonderful book community. It has been a pleasure getting to know you all.

As always, the biggest thank you to my parents for always believing in me and encouraging me to chase my dreams.

Also by Kaitlin Collins

The Falling Series

Falling for Scotland

Ringing in the New Year:
A Hogmanay Holiday Novella

Children's Lit

The Desk Dragon

About the Author

Kaitlin Collins is an elementary teacher and avid traveler based in the Kansas City, Missouri area. She lives with a menagerie of pets, including her bunny (Artemis), leopard gecko (Bruni), and puppy (Ringo). Books and writing have been her escape for years. When she isn't creating stories in her head, she's daydreaming about her next trip.

Instagram, Threads, and TikTok: @booksbykaitlin

You can also stay up to date on future projects by joining my Substack newsletter: The Collins Clan Gathering at https://booksbykaitlin.substack.com

www.ingramcontent.com/pod-product-compliance
Lightning Source LLC
Chambersburg PA
CBHW030235120726
47903CB00005B/1491